"*Speed Dreaming* is a book spilling over with talent. How enticing and accurately drawn these stories are, with their bright touches and ominous edges, their smart young characters blocked by what they can't see yet. A wonderful debut."

—Joan Silber, author of *Fools* and *Ideas of Heaven*

"Nicole Haroutunian's stories are precise little gems. I know I'll return to them again and again, since there's something new and beautiful to find in them every time I open this collection."

—Lauren Grodstein, author of *The Explanation for Everything*

"A bowler hat, a volleyball net, a pig tattoo: Nicole Haroutunian's stories all have unexpected details that attract the eye and alert the mind. Those details glitter on the surface while something else entirely goes on underneath: dark tides of life, death, illness, and love, and people who are carried away by them during the course of otherwise normal lives."

—Ben Greenman, author of *The Slippage* and *Mo' Meta Blues*

"An unforgettable portrait of what it's like to be a young woman in contemporary America . . . A beautiful, funny, and unflinching collection."

—Saïd Sayrafiezadeh, author of *Brief Encounters with the Enemy*

"The world of *Speed Dreaming* is populated by women who are stronger than they think they are. The moments in which they catch a glimpse of their true strength—and there is one in each of these twelve dazzling, linked stories—are tiny explosions of magic. Nicole Haroutunian is a magician, and this a stellar debut."

—Shelly Oria, author of *New York 1, Tel Aviv 0*

"The characters who appear (and reappear) in *Speed Dreaming* are full of intelligence, wit, and empathy—as well as regret, fickleness, and occasional selfishness. In other words, they are wholly human. With unbelievable precision and grace, Nicole Haroutunian examines the exquisite, transcendent, and inexplicably eerie moments of her characters' everyday lives and gives meaning to the smallest details of their worlds. *Speed Dreaming* is unforgettable."

—Nelly Reifler, author of *Elect H. Mouse State Judge*

"These passionate stories of women and their half disasters, half-rotten men, and fully open hearts are written so nimbly and with such energy and momentum and compassion that I found myself carrying the book from room to room, brushing my teeth and feeding the dog while reading, unwilling to put them down."

—Deb Olin Unferth, author of *Revolution: The Year I Fell in Love and Went to Join the War*

"Nicole Haroutunian is a master of excavating what is ominous and therefore worthy of examination in our everyday lives—sleepover games, damaged bodies, dying cities, Brooklyn parrots, and the prosaic catastrophes of love. I loved reading these perfectly formed stories about thoughtful urbanites and their search for meaning in the mundane."

—Amy Shearn, author of *The Mermaid of Brooklyn* and *How Far Is the Ocean from Here*

"Nicole Haroutunian's debut is a stunning speed dream in itself. These propulsive stories of young women in and out of love, work, and trouble are suffused with a strange magic that lingers long after the final page has been turned."

—Dawn Raffel, author of *The Secret Life of Objects*

"Fire, accidents, mysterious disease, and a coyote at a child's birthday party are only some of the calamities that these protagonists must confront, along with the minor indignities and incongruities of romance and work. Haroutunian brings her complicated young women to life with utter literary confidence. A splendid debut."

—Melvin Jules Bukiet, author of *Undertown* and *A Faker's Dozen*

"These honest and perceptive stories contend with the painful contradictions of modern love: that it is precious as it is quotidian, inadequate as it is essential."

—Julie Sarkissian, author of *Dear Lucy*

SPEED DREAMING

STORIES

SPEED DREAMING

STORIES

NICOLE HAROUTUNIAN

Little
a

Versions of stories in this collection have appeared in *Two Serious Ladies*, the *Literarian*, *Barnstorm*, *Day One*, and *Vol. 1 Brooklyn*.

Published by Little A, New York
www.apub.com

Amazon, the Amazon logo, and Little A are trademarks of Amazon.com, Inc., or its affiliates.

ISBN-13: 9781612184968
ISBN-10: 1612184960

Cover design by Merideth Mulroney

Library of Congress Control Number: 2014948838

Printed in the United States of America

For my family

Contents

SPEED DREAMING

STORIES

THE LIVING

O n her first night in New York City, in the furnished apartment high on the Upper East Side, where her savings would allow her six months' rent, Sabrina took a bath and studied the way her ribs were now countable through her skin. She wrapped her hair in a towel and ordered dinner from a menu she'd found slipped under her door.

A teenager delivered her food. He was overdue for a haircut, but his face was still smooth. She liked that Thai restaurants were staffed by Thai people here. When he gave her the price, she was shocked until she remembered that, in New York, everything counts twice. She said as much and, as he reached into his pocket for her change, he replied, "But you only live once."

The banality of his statement struck her, and she let out a bleat of laughter. If he'd waited an instant longer to turn away, she would have told him.

When Sabrina awoke the next day, her studio awash in morning light, the confession was still there like a catch in her throat, threatening escape. At the diner on the corner, staring at the bowl of yogurt and granola in front of her, she said, "It was silly to have gotten something so healthy."

The waitress, a woman about her age with a sleeve of tattoos and a cute, campy apron, said, "Next time, think about the peanut butter pancakes."

Admiring the red Formica tables and chrome stools around her, Sabrina thought that six months is not long except when measured in breakfasts: 180, maybe 184. "I'll keep that in mind," she said. This wasn't the place to make awkward admissions, not if she'd be back. She could die *now* thinking about it. Then she asked, "Where do you like to shop?"

It was a jewel box of a boutique hung with only ten different dresses. If she were the size she was a year ago, none of them would have fit, but now she had her pick. The shopgirl zipped her into an off-white silk sheath with a slit down the middle of the back. "It's perfect," the girl said. "The color is gorgeous with your red hair. Is it for any particular occasion?"

Sabrina smoothed her hands over her hips, felt their sharpness through the liquid fabric. "Yes," she said. Her nose tickled as if she were about to sneeze. "It's because I'm sick."

The girl smiled. "It's nice to get yourself a little pick-me-up when you're under the weather."

"I'm not under the weather," Sabrina said, searching for the right phrase. "More like *six feet* under." Her head was rushing, and she saw, looking down, the dress fluttering with the beating of her heart. The shopgirl's hands stopped fussing at her neckline.

"I'm so sorry," she said, folding her arms across her stomach. She was just as skinny as Sabrina, although she must have worked hard at it—spin class, salad dressing on the side.

"You really think the dress looks nice?" Sabrina asked, pulling cash from her wallet.

The shopgirl nodded, her eyes dancing around the room.
"I'll wear it out."

The spring wind rippled the silk across Sabrina's skin as she took herself to the park, to the café on the library steps beside it, and ordered
a glass of white wine. The green was crowded with coworkers lunch-
ing and mothers towing dizzy children away from the small merry-
go-round beside it. Her wine arrived, and she sipped with relief.

"Are you cold?" asked the man sitting a table over. He wore a
navy suit and a checked button-down shirt. He had been eating a
salmon salad and taking business calls on his cell phone. When he
put it down, Sabrina saw that he had a nick in his ear, a small trian-
gular piece missing in the lobe. She imagined what it might feel like
to fit her fingertip into that space.

Sabrina was shivering, her arms and legs dappled with goose
bumps. She saw how this could go—the identities she could assume,
now that she was the kind of frail beautiful girl that ruled this city,
now that she was free to spend the rest of her money on clothes that
completed the picture. There would be no one to dispute whatever
lies she might tell. She had been, on some level, preparing herself
for this. There was the dress, the care she'd taken to keep her hair, at
least, looking healthy. The businessman's eyes matched his suit, and
she had no doubt that he would buy her a drink and lift her dress to
her waist in any dark midtown corner.

"No, I'm not cold. Just very sick," she said. Either it was the wine
or she was feeling brave. "I'm going to die."

He drew his drink closer to his chest. He would not pay her bill now.

Over the next few weeks, she proved herself correct—she could have
someone every night, if she kept quiet until it was over. She liked the
sex, really liked it, for the first time in her life, and sometimes, she
liked the men. There was one she lingered with too long, a sweet man

named Ellis; before she told him, he asked to see her again. He made her forget only to remember.

She was already living so many lives in the hearts and minds of those she loved back home. There was a notepad where she kept track of the stories she invented for them when they called or wrote, which they did, except for the boyfriend she missed so little she could only think there had been one small blessing in all of this. She focused on small pleasures—extravagant coffee drinks at the diner in the morning and pricey salon blowouts once a week, movies during the day and tours at every museum up and down Fifth Avenue—and when the day accumulated into too heavy a burden, she would share it. To the docent at the Met, she'd say, "I'm so glad I got to do this before I die." To the teenager plucking her banana pudding from the bakery case, she'd ask, "Is it good enough for a last meal?" To the operator of that merry-go-round in the park, she said, "Just one more time around before . . ."

It was the elderly ticket taker at the art house cinema who clutched her arm—which finally had slimmed beyond attractiveness—and said, "Me too."

When Sabrina felt the pads of the woman's fingers on her skin, it was really bone on bone. What first appeared to be dyed-dark hair was a wig; the carefully arched eyebrows were drawn in. To be old! Sabrina wanted to push her, to watch her fall.

But how sad, how shrunken, how alone she seemed. Who could endure it for so long?

Leaving the movie, Sabrina followed a raw screeching sound down a cobbled street and through a warehouse door. A black-clad band was playing on a makeshift stage, which seemed about to buckle under. The three men in the band looked like giants, filling the room with their scowling confidence. The audience was elastic—surging forward, then receding. The men, rangy and sleeveless, had dirty shoulders; the few women, in shorts and tights, had defiant eyes. Sabrina's bones hurt under the assault of the relentless music. The air was sour with spilled beer and damp with sweat. She felt more light-headed than usual. The T-shirts tacked to the wall announced that the band was called Sacrament.

In a lull, as the drummer searched for a replacement for his splintered stick, Sabrina waded into the crowd. The riotous noise started again. When the first person struck her side, she stumbled, turned a heel. A pair of tattooed arms broke her fall and sent her hurtling backward, where she was caught again. Her hair came loose, and she flung it from shoulder to shoulder. She launched herself forward. She was breathless; the unmistakable taste of blood filled her mouth. But no matter how hard she was hit, she stayed standing.

The next time she went to the movies, Sabrina accepted the ticket taker's invitation to sneak in for a second film. Jeanne's shift was over, and she wanted to watch, too.

The movie was incomprehensible. The dim screen was no more than a shifting pattern of light, a glimpse of outer space or the ever after. Jeanne slipped low in her chair, head lolling before coming to rest on Sabrina's shoulder. It was a while before the warmth of Jeanne's body traveled through the plastic bulk of her wig to Sabrina. She held still and took it in: the heat, the small fluctuations of breath, the living. When Jeanne roused herself at the end of the film, she gave Sabrina a business card.

"He's the very best," Jeanne said.

"That window opened and shut without my knowing," Sabrina said as they walked out, rubbing her thumb across the raised print, the doctor's Park Avenue address. "All I have are these." She jiggled her purse, and in the silence of the credits, they could hear the pain pills rattle.

Jeanne held out her hand, and Sabrina dispensed. "Tell me you had a second opinion," Jeanne said.

"Hearing it once was enough," Sabrina said. "I didn't want to waste time. I always wanted to live in New York."

Jeanne reached out and tapped her manicured nail on the card. "Make an appointment," she said. "You are here to *live* in New York."

Years later, Sabrina has stopped searching for Jeanne in every new waiting room, at every new doctor's office. When she goes to the movie theater, in the moment after they kill the lights, before the film glows to life, she sees Jeanne's face, yes, but not only hers. She sees the shopgirl; the businessman with the salmon salad; Ellis, who asked to see her again. Take my pain, she'd told them, reckless and thin. She wonders, always will, if they did.

YOUSE

O n the morning of this newest test—didn't they just have one?—
Margaret slips her foot from its canvas shoe, extends her leg
from the knee, and brushes her toes up the calf of the boy in front
of her, Erik Paley. She feels his muscles flex. He shifts his back so
his paper is visible to her. Erik only gets Bs, but she could do worse.
He always pops a piece of gum in his mouth before they meet after
school on test days—thoughtful for a ninth grader, really.

She'd be more inclined to try the test on her own if she hadn't
discovered yesterday that she was screwing up in English, too. She'd
had no idea until Ms. Helmsley handed her last essay back with an
appointment time rather than a grade on it; she has to go see the
guidance counselor after geometry today.

When she gets there, Mr. Bertino has a photocopy of the essay.
Margaret doesn't like the idea of her work proliferating without her
knowledge. How many other copies are out there?

"Your teacher is concerned about your subject matter, Margaret,"
he says.

"But she gave me a choice," Margaret says. "For independent study,
when I wasn't coming to school."

"Sylvia Plath brings up some very serious—"

"I'm not going to kill myself," she says. "I know girls get obsessed with her. My mother already made fun of my unoriginality. But it's not like I wrote about how she put her head in an oven."

In truth, Margaret hadn't been familiar with Sylvia Plath when she chose her essay topic; she just saw a poem entitled "Daddy" in an anthology and went with it. The poem was pretty unsettling, actually—it wasn't the best portrait of a father-daughter relationship—but her paper would have been late if she'd had to find something else.

"What's the rest of your class reading now?" Mr. Bertino asks.

"Dickens," she says.

"Time for you to get back on track," he says. "Whether it be the best of times or the worst."

At lunch, Margaret and Joanna sit on a ledge outside the plate glass cafeteria windows.

"My mom refuses to acknowledge that I don't eat this stuff," Margaret says, peeling pink slices of roast beef from between lettuce leaves and white bread. "She thinks that I'm trying for anorexia with this vegan thing, but I swear. If she'd seen that film we saw . . ."

"My mother is thrilled I only want vegetables," Joanna says. Her lunch consists of carrot sticks and celery sticks, with a small Tupperware of fat-free Italian dressing for dipping.

"You're beautiful," Margaret tells her, and she is—greenish eyes, dark hair, curves for days.

"I do think we're onto something," Joanna says. "It's healthier to be vegan, too. My hips are going down for sure, and my boobs even—they look smaller, right?"

They don't. "Maybe," Margaret says. "I think my skin's improving."

"Know it," Joanna says.

They watch the action on the other side of the window like they're at the movies. "What if we sat with the Chinese kids one day?" Margaret muses. "Would they let us?"

"You never hear about that," Joanna says. "It's always black kids versus white kids. Where's the news special on white kids versus Chinese kids?"

"Let's try to hook up with one," Margaret says.

"By one, you mean a Chinese kid?" Joanna says.

"Yes, sorry."

Joanna affects a solemn expression, eyes wide. Margaret's begun to recognize these looks.

"Is this about your dad?" Joanna asks quietly.

"I never wanted to make out with my dad." Margaret folds soggy lettuce into her mouth.

"Because he died in China," Joanna says. "Is that why you care suddenly about the Chinese kids?"

Margaret's father had his aneurysm in China, it was true. He was there to research an article about a dissident, an artist who embroidered her own skin with silk thread. Margaret found out afterward that he knew it could happen at any time; he'd had his first aneurysm when he was in his twenties, soon after he met her mother. There was a little bomb in his brain. China didn't set it off; it just went on its own.

Margaret squeezes her bread into a ball and tosses it at the trash can. It hits the window instead. Ms. Washington, the new reading specialist stuck with lunch-monitor duty, starts toward them but stops when she recognizes Margaret.

"All I'm saying," Margaret explains, "is that we could be part of the solution rather than the problem."

Margaret can hear the little kids playing in the park: the thump of their feet against the rubber under the jungle gym, their screeching after-school mania. Erik, who is often late to class, is never late to meet her here behind the handball court. At the beginning of the year, he'd been shorter than she was, but now he's caught up. She hopes they'll be done with all of this by the time he's taller than her, but if that means starting to understand math again, she's not sure she can end it.

As far as Margaret knows, Joanna's the only other person aware of this arrangement. Before her father died, Erik probably would have told everyone, but she has a bit of a pall on her now. No one makes fun of her, thank goodness, but they talk to her less, stare at her more—she's constantly worried there's something in her teeth.

Today, things go a step further than usual: her hand ends up down Erik's pants, his waistband chafing against her wrist. She isn't quite sure what to do, but it doesn't seem to matter. His eyes are practically rolled back in his head.

After a few seconds, at a loss, she says, "I have to go."

He stares at her like he's dumb.

"See you later," she says.

Margaret heads straight to Joanna's house. Joanna's mother doesn't work because her little brother has autism and goes to tons of appointments and specialized programs. In the past, Margaret used to let herself into their house, look at Billy's toy trains with him, and chat with Laurie—Margaret calls her Laurie, not Ms. Greenbaum. Recently, she avoids visits like this for a few reasons. One, Billy is older now and less adorable. Two, Laurie constantly hugs Margaret's head and tells her that she's a good girl, which objectively she is not. Three, she can't help thinking about these changes the whole time she's there, which makes her feel and, she suspects, act weird.

She sits on the front steps for a few minutes, breathing in the sweet scent of leaf rot. The door swings open behind her. "Joanna is in the bathroom," Billy says. "Mom says come in."

Margaret turns around to smile at him, a smile he does not return. "I'd rather sit here," she says.

She hears Laurie calling from inside.

"Mom says . . ." Billy repeats.

"Okay, okay," she says.

Inside, Laurie's doing something strange involving spreadsheets. She has an overturned SnackWell's box next to her, and her hair is in a messy bun. She gestures Margaret over and squeezes her close, smelling like smoke.

"How are you, baby," she says. "How's mom."

Margaret hates when people ask questions that aren't. Laurie's voice doesn't elevate—she thinks she knows the answer, and she thinks that answer is bad.

"I did great on my math test today," Margaret says. "And my mother's firm just got a big commission. She'll probably get a promotion. What about you?" She gestures at the computer.

"Oh, this," Laurie says, drawing uncomfortably near to Margaret's ear. "Billy goes to junior high next year. We don't know where to send him, so I'm making a file of pros and cons of all of our options."

"He's lucky you have the time to do that," Margaret says, then regrets it when she sees Laurie wince. In truth, when she was younger, Margaret often wished that her mother didn't work, that she was around as much as Joanna's. There were months when she had dinner at Joanna's house more often than her own. Her father would pick her up at nine at night and tease that maybe she should just move in there, for all the time he got to see her.

Joanna appears, hands clenched over her abdomen. "Kill me," she says.

Her mother hands her three Advil. "Exercise," she says. "I know you want to curl into a ball, but I swear nothing helps more than exercise."

They head outside. Margaret suggests jumping jacks, but Joanna says she'd rather take a walk.

"Should we tell your mom?" Margaret asks.

Joanna rolls her eyes. "She'll try to come with us or something."

After a few blocks, they come to the town's main street, Broadway. Margaret's been to the real Broadway, an hour north—she can take or leave the musicals, but she loves the sugary coconut cubes her dad used to buy her from the street vendors—and so it seems ridiculous to call this street by the same name. Its big attractions are a grocery store, the pharmacy that fills everyone's prescriptions, a TCBY, and three gas stations, because everyone has to drive out of town to get anywhere good.

As they pass the yogurt shop, Margaret says, "I will say I miss the cookie dough," but her voice is drowned out by the honking of a passing bronze SUV. The man inside yells, "How about youse sit on my dick?"

"Did he say 'youse'?" Margaret asks, shuddering.

Joanna rubs her arms as if she's showering. "Dirty," she says. "Bad grammar makes me feel dirty."

"I bet he's married," Margaret says.

"My dad never believes me when I say that men do that. He can't conceive of it."

"Can you imagine your dad yelling out his car at teenage girls?"

"Can you imagine yours?" Joanna turns red instantly. "That's the worst thing I've ever said."

"I forgive you," Margaret says. "I don't know if God will, but . . ."

"Come on," Joanna says. "Get even. Say something terrible to me."

"I think I gave Erik Paley a hand job today."

Joanna stops dead. "Excuse me?"

"Loosely defined," Margaret says. "Nothing got sticky."

Joanna doubles over, gagging. "You're kidding me, right?"

"I mean, he let me cheat off of his test again . . ."

"You're killing me, Meggie," Joanna says. "You need to be on Prozac. You're not even into Erik."

"Not my finest hour, I agree."

"Next time that dude drives by," Joanna says, "let's make sure he knows that one of us is a pro."

Margaret cannot stay awake. Because she loved *Sense and Sensibility*, she thought old books were her new thing, but the Dickens is like a sedative. It hits her in the face every time she drifts off, the musty smell getting right up into her nose. She's reading the copy from her parents' bookshelf rather than the one from Ms. Helmsley. She'd be fooling herself to think that it was her father's copy—nonfiction was his thing—but her mother denies the book is hers. Her thing is minimalism; she never thinks twice about trucking decorative bowls or books or sweaters she hasn't worn in a year over to the Goodwill. People meeting her now might think she's dressing like she's in mourning, but she has always worn black: dresses with interesting cuts and modest hemlines, well fitting and lint-free. Margaret thought this was all very unusual until her mother brought her to work once and she realized all architects look the same. There was even one woman with hair a little shorter, lips a little redder, neckline a little more angular—her mother in sharper focus.

Rather than read, Margaret decides to try minimalism herself. She grabs some garbage bags and starts to tear down posters from her wall. As soon as she strips off the first one—a picture of a sour-looking cat, captioned "I *am* smiling"—she can't believe she's been looking at it for so long. She peels all her magazine clippings and song lyrics from the walls, breaking her thumbnail scratching off the stubborn shards of Scotch tape they leave behind. Then she sweeps half-empty bottles of old perfume, a collection of owl-shaped candles, and a miniature lava lamp off of her dresser and into a bag. Once she's discarded most of her clothing, leaving behind only one type of item in each color, she has enough drawer space to house the objects she doesn't want to completely forsake: a paperweight the green of an old Coke bottle; three photographs of her parents from their wedding day, her mother wearing white for possibly the only time ever, her father thinner and younger-looking than any married man should be; a colorful enamel box filled with all the jewelry

Margaret owns but never wears. Last in are the silver studs from her twelfth birthday, when her aunt signed off on six piercings in each ear, once for each year. She remembers how her parents, upon her triumphant return from the mall, demanded that all but two be removed.

She finds her Discman, inserts a mix from Joanna, and hits "Play" before carrying her full bags to the trash bins in the garage. Her mother is next door, in her own bedroom. Margaret has heard her crying in there only once, but she'll never forget the sound. It was worse than at the funeral, where they were all sobbing, of course. Margaret doesn't know if it was worse than when her mother got the phone call at work. She doesn't know what that scene was like, if the other black-dressed woman hugged her, what the men in their rectangular plastic glasses might have said. It had to have been worse than what she heard coming from the other side of the bedroom door. And it had to have been the door that made it seem this way, but part of what was so terrible about it was how quiet it was. For something like that, her mother should have been wailing, top volume, but she wasn't. She seemed a hundred miles away, drowning on the other side of an ocean.

At first, Margaret was upset that her mother didn't tell her until she got home from school, that she kept those few new hours of grief for herself. Now that's she lived with it, though, Margaret's glad for that gift of time. She remembers sitting in math class, Erik Paley just another kid in front of her, ignoring the hum of her teacher's voice, confident that, when he got back from his trip her father would teach her what she needed to know.

She showers before settling back down onto her bedspread, a dizzying patchwork quilt, which she will ask to exchange for a plainer one next time she's due for a gift. Wearing her one nightgown—she'd chosen the blue one to keep—in her nearly bare room, she concentrates, for three whole chapters, on reading *A Tale of Two Cities*.

Margaret raises her hand for every question during the first part of English class, but Ms. Helmsley seems to avoid calling on her, positioning her head so she can only see the other half of the room. Even after the Mr. Bertino visit, she'd refused to give Margaret a grade on that Sylvia Plath paper, which she'd called "inappropriate." Margaret thinks Ms. Helmsley's afraid that if she calls on her, Margaret will say something awkward. She wants to have an outburst to teach her a lesson until she thinks of what that would actually entail; she'd rather no one look at her than everyone. So she stuffs her worn novel into her shoulder bag and walks out of the room. She bets Ms. Helmsley won't call after her, and she bets right.

Joanna's in Spanish. Margaret pauses halfway down the hall. She closes her eyes and conjures the last time she saw her father. He was leaving for China early the next morning. At dinner, her mother apologized for ordering pizza instead of making something delicious.

"One thing I won't get over there is pizza," he said, ruffling her mother's perfectly straight hair—no one but her dad would ever dare to do that. "This is great."

Margaret had interrupted to ask about ordering one without mozzarella next time, because who knew how the cows were being treated. She'd banged her fist on the table when her parents exchanged a look, hating them for not taking her seriously.

She'd demurred from sharing dessert on the same grounds, although she can still picture the cheesecake—pillowy white with goopy cherry topping. She sulked through the sitcoms they watched before bed, even though they were her choice. No goodnight hug.

This does the trick, and by the time she knocks, she's wiping at real tears. Joanna's teacher comes to the door. "Can Joanna come see Mr. Bertino with me?" she asks.

Neither of them has cut school before. Their escape is complicated by the fact that they didn't think to stop at their lockers to grab their jackets before slipping out the side door of the gym and onto the grass behind the school. It's November, and the air is biting. "This limits where we can go," Margaret says, her breath visible.

"What's the plan, man?" Joanna asks. "I'm a little outside my comfort zone here."

"Let's walk to my house," Margaret says. "My mom won't be there. We'll get sweaters and figure out the next move."

They scurry through a thicket of trees onto the street, maintaining speed until they're a few blocks away, fairly confident they haven't been detected. Margaret expected they'd feel giddy, like thrill seekers, but they press ahead in silence.

"Are you mad?" she asks.

Joanna twists her ponytail around her finger, considering. "I will be if we get caught."

"Fair enough," Margaret says.

Then the bronze SUV—the same one, it has to be—is slowing down beside them. They hear a familiar voice. "How about youse . . . ?"

Margaret does not want to hear the rest of his sentence. "How about we fucking kill you?" she yells, kicking her foot in the direction of the car.

"I'm going to scream," Joanna murmurs. "Let's scream."

"No," Margaret says, walking faster as the man keeps pace. "We'll get in trouble if someone comes. He just wants attention—he's full of shit."

"What are you going to do?" the guy asks. His voice is threat and danger together, like when thunder and lightning happen at the same time. Margaret notes that he's dropped the "youse."

Joanna grabs for Margaret's wrist and starts off toward someone's yard. Margaret leans back in opposition. Their tug-of-war paralyzes them. It's not that Margaret's being stubborn by not changing course—it's that the yard is full of shrubs, shrubs she can picture lying dead in.

He rolls down the window a little further. Now no one is moving.

"I can see you," Margaret says, although she can't. "We memorized your freaking license plate!"

He says, "Oh yeah?" and then he pops open the passenger door. It swings so close it almost hits them.

Then they're running: Joanna through the yard and Margaret down the street, running how she does in dreams, without regard for what's beneath her feet, not knowing where she's headed, only that there's something to escape. In her dreams, it is unclear what that is—the terrifying unknown behind her—but now, she knows: it is a man in a car who has things he wants her to do.

She doesn't stop until she sees the SUV pass her. He's leaning on the horn, picking up speed until he screeches through a stop sign at the end of the block, peeling off into the distance. She thinks to look at his license plate for real but can't see it clearly through her tears. The relief as he disappears lasts only a moment before she realizes that Joanna might be in the car, disappearing with him.

Margaret is dashing toward the nearest house, yelling about 911, when a hand touches her shoulder. She screams, the person behind her screams, the older woman opening her front door screams. It is surround sound panic until Margaret turns to see Joanna standing there, leaves stuck to the side of her hair, but there, in the flesh, screaming, too.

Billy's wild for the story. The girls are rigid on Margaret's family room couch, knees together and mouths set. Their mothers are bidding good-bye to the police at the front door, extracting promises that what can be done will be done, but Billy's pacing around the house, assembling facts, a one-man crime-fighting machine. He's having the best day of his life.

Margaret watches him zooming in circles and scribbling on a notepad and says, "I can't believe that a letter is going out to everyone."

"Who cares that our names won't be in it," Joanna says. "It'll be obvious."

"Last time a letter like that went out, some weirdo had offered candy to a first grader. An effing first grader. We're not some helpless little freaks."

"Who'll make out with us now?" Joanna says.

"Everyone," Margaret says. "The letter's an advertisement that we're the kind of girls who cut class and get into dumb situations. Everyone will make out with us, but no one will talk to us."

"You know all about that," Joanna says.

Margaret flinches. "It's not so bad, in the end," she says.

"I'm going to transfer to that Jewish day school."

"I'll die without you," Margaret says.

"I think we've established," Joanna says, "that we don't really stick together in life-or-death situations."

Billy hustles over and says, "I have a few more questions for the investigation."

"You're up," Margaret tells Joanna, heading for her bedroom. She pulls the quilt from her bed and throws it into the near-empty closet. She stands there for a second before climbing in after it, burying her head in the soft folds.

In the park the next day, Erik asks, "So you didn't get a good look at the guy's face?"

"He was just a guy."

"What do you think he wanted with you?"

Margaret pulls back, putting some air between her face and Erik's pointed chin. He has grown—she's sure of it—his chin is now level with her bottom lip. "Same thing you want," she says.

He shakes his head, his fine hair flapping around his ears. "I don't want anything," he mumbles.

"Do you want to come over?" Margaret asks. "My mom's not home."

"I have homework," he says. "Homework. You should try it."

As she walks home, Margaret thinks that if the SUV reappeared, she'd get in. What's the worst that could happen?

It's almost disappointing when nothing does. It's obvious that she's not speaking to Joanna, so Margaret has to make up a stream of lies to her mother about what she's doing with her time after school. Pretending this person or that is driving her home, she manages to make the journey alone every day that week, walking, each day more slowly than the last. On Friday, she even paces in front of her house for a while, until the sun sets and she worries that the SUV actually *will* appear. Inside the house, she pulls out her quilt and drags it over to the couch, where she considers starting her homework. She's behind again, which is one of the reasons, Mr. Bertino told her mother, she didn't get suspended for cutting.

A knock on the door startles her. She dials 9-1- and, finger poised at the final digit, creeps toward the door. The silhouette through the peephole is terrifying until she recognizes the shape, the mass of curly hair.

Margaret opens the door. "Tell me you didn't walk here in the dark."

Joanna points at the idling car, her whole family watching them through the windows.

"We're on our way to dinner," she says. "I wasn't going to call you, but I didn't see you at lunch or after school, like, all week. I wanted to make sure you weren't, you know."

"Dead in the trunk of a car," Margaret supplies. "I did go to the cafeteria for a second on Tuesday."

"You didn't wind up eating in the bathroom?" Joanna says, squinting as if looking for the germs.

"I did," Margaret says, squinting back.

"We aren't in a fight, right?" Joanna asks.

Margaret shakes her head. "Just a break, I guess."

Joanna holds up a finger, letting her family know she's on her way. "In your absence," she says, "I've been sitting with the Chinese kids."

"What's that like?" Margaret asks.

Joanna shrugs. "You'll have to see for yourself."

Over dinner—pizza, no cheese—Margaret's mother says she's glad she and Joanna are talking again. She takes a sip of wine. "You go days without speaking to me, you know."

"Do not," Margaret says.

"You don't notice. But I do."

Margaret takes a huge bite of pizza so she won't have to respond. She worries that there's more coming—an indictment about her purging her room, perhaps, or some sort of ninja knowledge about her math-test cheating. But her mother just sits there staring, eyes and nose red around the edges. She looks like she's been outside in the cold.

Margaret swallows. She reaches across the table for her mother's hand, her thin hand with red nail polish, which Margaret is surprised to see is chipped.

"Just a sip," her mother says, and pushes her glass of wine into Margaret's waiting palm.

PILGRIMS

Dax has a pig tattooed on his arm, and its rump flexes as he jerks the steering wheel. We're careening down a single lane in Wales, fields on either side of us, six-foot-tall embankments lining the road. He's never driven on the wrong side of the street before, and he doesn't have a handle on where car ends and dirt wall begins. Every couple of yards, a warning alarm shrieks and he veers to the right, bouncing off that side instead. Grasses protrude from the mud-streaked hood of the rental car, gathering as we go.

I breathe steady. I'm not usually prone to motion sickness, but now my stomach is churning. I look at the pig rather than out the window. It's bright with a sheen of sweat; Dax is driving fast to cover his nerves. The side of my thumb is wrinkled and pink from biting.

But when we take a bend on two wheels and come face-to-face with a tractor, what is there to do but scream?

Our heads hit our seat backs as we stop short. The driver is shouting something at us, but his Welsh accent is impenetrable. Dax's hair is damp at the nape of his neck, and his nose twitches. He cranes forward, trying to understand what the man is saying.

"My best guess is 'Back up,'" I say, lifting myself by my elbows to look behind us, swallowing the sour taste in my mouth. There is a half-moon turnoff a little ways back.

"Why doesn't *he* back up?" Dax says. "You back up!" He gestures at the man with his fist.

The man—he must be a farmer—emerges from his tractor. He wears beige twill pants, navy rubber waders and a plaid button-down. I'd guess him to be about forty-five. "He doesn't look like he wants to fight," I say.

"Well, I might," Dax says, stepping out of the car. He approaches the farmer with his chest puffed out in defiance. The farmer looks down at him from his substantial height.

Dax is built like a rectangle. He has a dark beard that could absorb a punch. I can't imagine him knocked over or knocked out. I've seen him in verbal altercations before, and I've heard stories about his hotheaded past. But he knows, or I think he knows, what I would and would not abide.

I gnaw on my thumb, watching the conversation. A conversation, though, is all it seems to be. No yelling, no more fist shaking. Then Dax is headed back to the car, striding with purpose. "We're following him to his place for lunch."

His place is a true farmhouse. It is two stories, built of weatherworn stone blocks. The roof is slanted and battered, but the shutters are painted fresh butter yellow. There are great iron hinges on the front door, and the windows are made of mottled blown glass. The yard immediately surrounding the house is populated with hundreds of thousands of round pebbles in beige, peach, and pink. Beyond that, there are the fields—cows and sheep calling back and forth across them.

Dax and I wait beside our car, rolling our feet on the pebbles as the farmer situates his tractor by an outbuilding. A wizened brown dog trots over to him as he dismounts. "How's this for local color," Dax whispers, as if this jaunt were in his plans all along.

The fresh air is a salve for my nausea. I pull my denim jacket close to my chest, the June breeze in Wales as cool as our New York April. I've been trying to tamp down my disappointment about how wrong this trip has been so far; I don't want to give myself away by seeming too pleased that something seems to be going right.

The farmer approaches me, hand extended. "Alwyn," he says.

"Thanks so much for having us, Alwyn," I say. "I'm Meg."

"Meg!" he exclaims. "Welsh, then? Or Irish?"

"No, no." I shake my head. "My mother just liked the name."

He claps me on the back, guiding us toward the house. "As soon as I saw you on the road, I thought, ah—company. My wife went shopping just this morning, so we should have plenty to eat."

"Please don't feel obligated to feed us."

He waves me off and says something else, but I can't decipher it through his thick, jocular brogue. I make a note to research if "brogue" pertains only to the Irish or to those on this side of the sea, too. I steal a glance at Dax. He shakes his head; he's far worse with accents than I am.

Alwyn throws open the farmhouse door. His wife is standing just on the other side. She doesn't back up as we enter, so we end up uncomfortably close. I can't tell if she means her slightly open arms as a welcoming gesture or if she's blocking us, protecting her home. She's in her early thirties—nearer our age than Alwyn's—and pregnant, her stomach pushing the limits of her linen shift. Her hair is dark, streaked with gray at the temples, and her eyes are the blue green of the seawater we were headed toward before our run-in. I've never seen skin like hers, poreless, punctuated by a network of dark moles that make the pale paler.

"Eira, I've brought you some Americans," Alwyn announces, giving her a big, blustery kiss on the cheek before sweeping her aside and motioning for us to enter.

"I hope we're not intruding," I say. The wide wooden floorboards are intermittently covered with the most beautiful woven rugs. They're patterned with red and white diamonds, a rugged warp and weft. I don't want to step on them, fearing mud on my boots. Dax stands on one without a thought. When Eira turns to lead us into the house, I see his eyes on her, on the lovely shape of her legs from behind. I add a tick mark to the list in my head.

In the kitchen, the wooden ceiling beams hang low. A curtainless window looks over one of the fields, where cows swish their tails. The countertops are cracked white tile—cloudy, as if they'd been wiped down with a dingy rag. An ancient silver kettle hisses on the stove.

"I'll pour you some tea," Eira says. She looks at Dax, her eyes alight. "What is it, Americans don't take cream?"

He grins at her. "That's right," he says.

Dax, Alwyn, and I sit down at a picnic table behind the house and sip our bitter tea. "Can't I help her?" I ask, but Alwyn shakes his head.

"Guests are guests," he says. "What brings you here to our part of the world?"

I take a drink, waiting for Dax to explain. He says, "It was an accident."

Alwyn throws his head back in delight as Dax relays his British aunt's generous offer to let us use her neighbor's vacation rental for free. Dax arranged it all on his own, a traditional honeymoon—until we boarded the plane, I was in the dark. He'd told me to pack a bathing suit and sweaters. On the phone with friends, I contemplated destinations from California to Korea. Who could have guessed Bath? The town in the English countryside was achingly charming, built around a natural spring, where Brits like Jane Austen convalesced and took the waters. Dax had no idea I wrote my undergrad thesis on *Mansfield Park*, but he knew I'd love the idea of Bath, and I did. It wasn't until we arrived at the door to find another couple staying in our picturesque little house that we discovered his aunt had offered us the wrong home. The vacant one wasn't in Bath but near the coast of Wales, five winding hours' drive from civilization. We tried to find another place to stay, but costs were prohibitive. A few hours later, we were on the road. We'd arrived yesterday evening, too jet-lagged to explore. "We knew nothing about this place before we drove up," Dax says.

The Wales cottage isn't without charm, but it's spare and small, isolated from even the microvillages that dot the region. I couldn't stop thinking that Dax had bungled it. I'd been in charge of the wedding planning, which had been, not without grave effort, flawless. Setting out on our drive, he was ready to embrace an adventure, but I had to work to mask my resentment. He saw right through it, I'm sure, but who wants to be a jerk on honeymoon? I affect a smile. "So far, we know that there are cliffs, the Irish Sea, and very narrow streets," I say.

"And *we* know," Alwyn says, "that you lot can't drive for shit!"

I expect Dax to bristle—he doesn't take well to teasing—but something about the Welsh air is agreeing with him. "You know the place we're staying?" he asks, gesturing in the general direction.

"You're at Clyde's, then?" Alwyn says. "Nice place. Don't use the grill outside, though—sets off a smoke alarm. Renters always make that mistake and can't make it stop. I've gone over in my nightclothes before."

"All we've been eating are the yogurts and potato chips—crisps— we got on the road," I say. In truth, I hadn't minded that part. I hadn't allowed myself more than a handful of potato chips in years. We'd come across a brand that lists the sort of potato, as well as the farm in which it was grown, right on the bag.

"You're in for a treat, then," he says. "Eira is a brilliant cook."

She appears moments later, carrying a tray piled with ham sandwiches and flat currant-studded biscuits. The sandwiches are dry, nothing more than bread and meat. Alwyn gives them a quizzical look; Dax polishes his off in a few bites. I can barely swallow a few mouthfuls before they threaten to come back up.

Eira tucks a piece of hair behind her ear. "I'm sorry for the sandwiches," she says. "I was so involved in baking the Welsh cakes that I forgot about a proper lunch."

I take a cake and spread it with the lemon curd she's set out in a little dish. It is warm, not too sweet, divine. "I could eat a hundred," I tell her, although I take only two. "This is perfect—thank you."

"I liked the ham, too," Dax says, flashing the pig on his arm. "Can't go wrong."

"He's a butcher," I explain.

"Don't butcher mine!" Alwyn cries, pointing his thumb toward his flock of sheep. I understand his joke on the third try and translate it for Dax.

"But I'm sure they'd be delicious, raised here," he says.

Wanting to draw her into the conversation, I ask Eira how far along she is.

"Six and a half months." She looks pointedly at my stomach. "And what about you?"

I start, drawing my hands over my middle. It's flat, perfectly flat. Heat rises in my cheeks and reddens to a burn. Dax stops chewing, a Welsh cake suspended in the air.

"Eira," Alwyn says. "Leave them be with all of that."

"I have a gift, usually," she says, meeting my eyes. "But I can't always be right."

Although I don't turn to look at him, I feel Dax next to me, his own heat vibrating across the space between us. There is no right way for me to react, so I try not to react at all. As much as I want to, I can't deny it.

Alwyn touches my shoulder. "Would you like to meet one of the lambs?" he asks, nodding over his shoulder at a rickety wooden barn.

"Please," I say. As Dax and Eira start to clear the table, I follow Alwyn over a loamy patch of grass, the brightest green. I feel like

I might vomit, but try my hardest not to; the timing is less than fortuitous.

I look back over my shoulder at Dax, trying to read him from behind. He balances the dishes on his forearm like the pro he is. He keeps pace with Eira, although his posture is stiff to prevent dropping the plates. It isn't often that I wish we knew each other better. I love that we were engaged in less than a year, the romance of simply believing in our connection, but now I can't help feeling a gap. We've never really talked about children. I don't know what he's thinking.

Inside the small damp building, the ceiling barely clears Alwyn's head. A white lamb sits on a bed of hay, four spindly legs folded beneath its tiny, trembling body. Alwyn lifts it and places it into my waiting arms. It has the sentient face of an old man with its searching, shiny eyes, long nose, and downturned mouth. Its ears are petal shaped, tender, and soft. I stroke its nubby fur, which yellows near its belly.

"Why is this lamb in here, away from the others?" I ask.

Alwyn shakes his head. "He enjoys your company."

I rock the lamb. Its breathing sounds labored, wet; I assume Alwyn sidestepped my question because it's sick. Is it going to die? He probably wouldn't tell me if it was. "Don't mind Eira," Alwyn says. "She fancies that she's descended from Druids, that she has some of their magic. It's probably true."

He says something else that I don't understand and reaches to take back the lamb. I'm hesitant to give it to him, to relinquish the feel of its warm, quick pulse against my chest. I ask him to repeat what he said. He shakes his head, but I press until we both relent. I let him take the lamb, and he says, "Nothing says magic makes you kind."

Back at the farmhouse, Dax has his sleeves rolled up as he dries the dishes. Eira rests against the counter, her left toe touching Dax's heel. Some women are at their most beautiful when pregnant. Sunlight angles in through the window, diffused by the waver in the glass. She is ethereal; the light isn't falling on her so much as emanating from her skin.

"You're like a Vermeer," I say. "What is it, *The Milkmaid*?"

They both look up, startled, and her face darkens. She must not know the painting.

"We should let you get back to work," Dax says.

Alwyn sighs. "Not doing me any favors, but it is about that time. Eira, maybe you can show them around for a bit?"

"No," I say. "We don't want to take any more of your day."

"Eira was telling me about these ruins up on the cliffs," Dax says. "The place where Saint David was born."

"I'll take you to see it," she says. "If you'd like. Let me just use the loo and get ready."

As Eira heads up the stairs, Alwyn bids us good-bye, joking again about running into us and shaking our hands. I keep my grip on his for a beat too long, willing him to stay, but the time comes to let go, and he goes. I cross my arms, stepping into an uneasy silence beside Dax.

"I don't want to spend any more time with her," I whisper.

"We can't back out," he hisses, although we could, of course. But he doesn't want to be alone with me as much as I don't with him.

"When were you going to tell me?" he asks.

"Honestly," I say, biting my thumb, "I don't know if it's true."

"But it might be," he says. "I keep thinking about it. We haven't been very careful."

"It might be, yes. I haven't taken a test." A couple of months ago, because of a medication conflict, I skipped a cycle of birth control pills and lost five pounds right away. I couldn't risk the weight returning before the wedding, so I haven't started them again yet.

"Meg, we're married now," Dax says. "No secrets."

I can't help noticing that he focuses on the deception, or the omission, rather than the possibility in this situation. "How about the way you're looking at Eira?"

He snorts and plants his hands on his hips in a gesture that to me looks oddly feminine. "I'm not looking at her like anything," he says. He keeps a careful distance. I'd rather he grab me, leave a bruise. "I mean, should we go home? Back to New York so you can see a doctor?"

"Oh, please," I say. "I'll just lay off the local pubs until we know one way or the other."

"You've been drinking," he says. "That's right." His gaze is even, but he's going haywire at the edges—the trembling corners of his mouth, the sweat gathering on his neck.

I push up my sleeves and fan my face. Dax's eyes skirt mine, landing on my stomach and then flickering away.

Eira reappears, rattling keys. "I'm driving," she announces.

I ride in the front, next to Eira. I can see a sliver of Dax in the side-view mirror, shoulder to elbow. Driving through the rural roads with Eira is different than having Dax at the wheel. We fly, but she knows what she's doing. At first, there isn't much to see. The embankments block all but the top of the wheat-colored grasses from view, and the sound of the wind coming through the cracked windows nearly blots out the braying sheep and the low-intoning cows. But soon there is a sense that we're rising through space, and then the sea is visible in front of us. It looks cold and deep. Its color changes in striations: white, glittering navy, luminous teal. Then we make a sharp left turn and start to drive along it.

"On a map," I say, "the distance between here and Ireland seems swimmable. I can't believe we can't see it."

"I've never been there," Eira says. "Not Alwyn either."

We turn away from the water and drive through one tiny town, then another. There are sprinklings of small houses, white-sided pubs, signs in both English and Welsh. Eira tells us that they're bilingual by law. "I've never seen so many *W*s," I say.

Before too long, we pull into a parking lot. It's more official than I was anticipating; there's even a small tourist center dispensing brochures. I'm surprised, and pleased, to discover that we aren't the only travelers around. I wonder if there actually might be a spa somewhere nearby. There are a handful of folks in sneakers and sweatshirts setting out on the paths at the same time we are. As soon as we start walking, though, Eira steps past the paved walkways and heads out into the green hills. She walks with brisk purpose, her gait seemingly unaltered by the weight of her belly. For a few yards, she pulls so far ahead of us that I wonder if she's forgotten we're here.

We hustle to catch up with her. The hem of my pants dampens and drags in the grass. Dax places his hand on my lower back to help propel me forward. The small gesture, a palm-sized connection, is a comfort.

After about five minutes of mad dash through the open air, we rejoin a path. No longer paved, it is compacted dirt, only wide enough for one. We fall into a soldier's march, Eira in front, Dax in the middle, me in the rear.

"Are we in a rush?" I ask.

Rather than answer, Eira extends a hand behind her. Dax takes it. Seeing them touch, it's as if they clutched me around my throat. I can see him leaving me as clear as the water below. I grab at his other hand and imagine jumping, being the weight that pulls the two of them off the path behind me, how lovely we'd all look falling through the sky.

What a mother I'll make.

We maneuver sideways along the ever-narrowing path, facing out. The hill rolls into a craggy precipice, then down to a ribbon of sandy beach, then the water.

In the distance, there is a series of splashes. "Whales?" I ask.

"There're loads of them," Eira says.

Dax drops our hands and points at the undulating humps and tails—"Whales in Wales!" he shouts. "Whales in Wales!" Despite his beard and the wrinkles around his eyes, he looks the way I imagine he must have as a child.

We keep up for another fifteen minutes until Eira winds us off the path again, turning away from the water. The air is clearer than it was even at the farm. Without the barnyard inflections, it is actually sweet. I wonder if that's why I'm not winded; I'm not usually one to exercise.

The ruins come into view with little warning; there is nothing but a small plaque to mark them. It says the building that once stood here was erected fifteen centuries ago. How many lifetimes is that? The patch of land it's on seems no different than any we had passed. It's a stone perimeter marking off an area of twenty feet by fifteen. The walls are knocked knee-high in places, stretching as tall as my shoulders in others. Wildflowers, purple and white, poke through porous spots between the stones. Within the walls, the floor is dirt and grass, the same inside as outside.

Eira hikes up her skirt as she steps over the lowest part of the wall. Facing us, she says, "I didn't want to chance anyone following us. There's another building over that way"—she points in the direction we came from—"that people get to and then they stop, thinking they've found Saint David's birthplace. What they've found is a chapel honoring him. It's very old and quite lovely, but it isn't this."

"What was his miracle?" I ask.

"He ministered in silence," she says. "But one day, he broke the silence to preach to a crowd, and while he spoke, a dove descended onto his shoulder. The land under his feet swelled, grew, until he rose above the people so they could all hear his message."

"So," I say, "the miracle was a hill?"

Eira blinks her wide eyes. "He also prayed to God that people should be warned when their loved ones were going to pass. He helped them know their own deaths."

She steps into the center of the ruins, sits, then spreads her body out flat to the ground. Gravity acts on her face, slackening her lips. Her hair has come undone and tangles around her head. Her dress falls across the rise of her stomach, riding up to expose her upper thighs. Being so close to her, lying in the same spot a woman once labored and gave birth to a saint, is nearly unbearable in its intimacy.

My breath catches; I hold my hand to my chest.

"I'm not looking," Dax says.

"How could you not?" I ask. I can't look away.

"This is strange," he says.

"Saint David's mother must have died, right?" I say. It's something I know, like I know now that magic isn't kind. "She must have died having him."

Eira is still, sunlight on her face. She's asleep or deep in a reverie. I back away from the ruins. Rather than retrace our steps, I continue up the path we were on. I clear the next hill before I turn to see if Dax is following me. Before long, the path leads us down to the beach.

"Should we go in?" Dax says.

I pull off my boots and roll up my jeans. We toe the surf, so cold it hurts. Dax is straight and stoic; he wades in up to his shins. He's watching for whales, but the horizon is still. I climb to a shelf of stone, drying my feet in the sun.

"Dax," I call to him. "Dax, it's too cold."

He turns back slowly, as if he's waking up. When he's close enough, I catch the corner of his shirt and pull him over next to me. He wraps an arm around my waist, his hand on my stomach. It rumbles under his touch.

"I'm starving," I say.

We make our way into town, our feet thawing on the walk, and pick up a big bag of food. A local we meet at the grocery store gives us a ride back to Alwyn and Eira's, where we fetch our car, tearing out onto the road in a spray of mud. In the long magic hours before it's completely dark at nearly eleven at night—Dax fires up the grill.

The cows and sheep call to each other across the fields. When the alarm sounds, I climb onto a chair and pull it off the wall.

VANDALS

Pushing a wheelchair is something I hope I never get good at, although I should at least try to get better.

"Sorry, honey," I say, after slamming him into a Purell stand.

He winces, rubbing his elbow. "Can't you at least aim for my legs?"

I bend to kiss the bruise but knock the elbow even harder. He shouts for Vicodin. His parents picked what seemed like a swank rehab center near their place out in New Jersey, but only about three people work here. We wait a while, but no one shows.

"What do you have to do to get medical attention around here, get hit by *another* truck?"

I ask.

He wants me to see some fish. There's a big aquarium in the back of the lobby filled with flashes of blue and yellow, orange and green. They are iridescent, otherworldly in their movements and their watchful silence. "Look into their eyes," Levi says. He gestures at a fish with an intellectual profile. Its mouth opens and closes as if there's a point it needs to get across. "Tell me you don't know guys like that," he says.

"I do," I admit.

There's a stretch of highway in New Jersey through a place that looks like a cross between an alien civilization and hell. I think it's called Elizabeth. Because I teach in Brooklyn most afternoons, I spend many a toxic hour stalled among those silos and generators, slogging between home, work, and the rehab center. I've already been in the car for three hours by the time I pull up to the elementary school. Does it get tiring? I feel like I've been hit by a truck.

At school, I've been tasked with introducing West African masks. It's a little delicate, given that the kids are mostly black and I am totally white. I assemble my first class of children around me on the rug. Ms. Bell, their teacher, settles in across the room, a pile of paperwork half obscuring her from view.

The kids love me for a few reasons. One, I'm in each classroom for just an hour and a half per week, so I don't see them enough to get frustrated and yell. Two, I don't see them enough to learn their names, so I call them all "sweetie" or "buddy"; en masse, I refer to them as "friends." Three, they get to call *me* by my first name, Tess, which only the boldest ones can do without giggling. Four, I think everything they do is wonderful.

"Why do people wear masks?" I ask.

"Protection," says one sweetie.

"Sports," says a buddy.

"Halloween?" tries a friend. This child is so large that I imagine he must have been left back at least twice. He assumes he is wrong when he answers questions, but luckily, that doesn't stop him from answering them.

"That's wonderful," I say. I check to make sure Ms. Bell is still grading and pull small palettes of face paint out of my tote bag, along with handheld plastic mirrors.

There are, of course, a couple of kids who can't handle the freedom. While everyone else is wonderful—painting whiskers beside their noses; horns on their foreheads; spots, stripes, and sports team logos onto their cheeks—these little outliers have a squabble over the mirror they're sharing and start to throw punches. Now Ms. Bell has to get involved, and her involvement, sadly, doesn't stop at removing the offenders.

"I can't send everyone to gym class with paint on their faces," she says.

I show her hypoallergenic baby wipes and assure her that she'll have her sweet-faced students back by period's end, but she demands they wash off immediately and gets on the phone with the teacher I have next. In her class, we make our drawings on paper. Cleanup's a snap, I'll give her that. I head back to New Jersey five minutes early.

"Do you still have any of the paint on you?" Levi asks.

"I do."

"Do me," he says.

"Happily," I say, reaching for the waistband of his pajama pants. Despite the injuries to his legs, other important things are still in working order. But we're never alone here to test them out. Sometimes I joke about wheeling us into a supply closet. "Oh, wait, you mean with the paint?"

He laughs, then clutches his ribs.

I went to college with someone who died young, this redhead who always got too drunk at parties, who once burned me on the arm with her flailing cigarette. She tried to keep it a secret when she got sick, but word got out. I wasn't in touch with her by then, but I heard it was something quick moving and awful. Imagine finding out you have only six months to live. Sometimes I see someone who looks like her on the street, and I wonder if it's still okay to laugh at the memories of her acting so crazy back when she was twenty.

And then there was this other kid, a neighbor from the cul-de-sac where I grew up, who sustained a head injury in a car crash that actually changed his personality. What he liked before, he didn't like anymore.

So I know how lucky we are that Levi is still here, that he's still Levi, but it's hard to feel it sometimes. I watch for a miracle out of the side of my eye, looking for a twitch in his toes, a knock in his knees.

When I first saw Levi, he was riding his bike past me as I walked to a party. The air literally moved around me. His muscular calves and the curve of his back, the way his knees were pumping—I couldn't help but hope that we were headed to the same place, even though, at the time, I was dating the party's host.

I paint white onto Levi's lips and around them in an *O*, then outline them in black. I use my fingernails to dab small *C* shapes up and down his stubbled cheeks, then shade his eyes so it looks like they're bulging. I pass him a mirror. "Do you get it?" I ask.

He opens and closes his mouth, fish-faced.

That night, when I brush my teeth, I notice a faint transfer of fish scales on my chin. I climb into bed and stare at the ceiling. I know I won't be able to sleep if I can't come up with that poor dead girl's name. I call Rico, this boyfriend I had back in college. We still talk from time to time. Levi has no idea.

"The redhead was Angela," Rico says. "We hooked up."

"Before or after me?" Knowing him, the answer is probably "during."

"It's funny you're calling," he says.

"Because you were just dreaming about me?"

"I am now," he says. "What are you up to?"

"Having a drink," I tell him, because what am I going to say: I'm wearing sweatpants?

He asks if I want to come meet him and tells me the bar he's at. I say I'll see him there and pull Levi's cool pillow to my chest. I like picturing Rico watching the door, waiting for me.

As I fall asleep, I think that Angela wasn't her name at all.

The next morning, there's nothing but a ball of wrinkled sheets in Levi's bed. I clutch the door frame. For a moment, looking at his bed,

I just know that he's dead. Right after the accident, he had a surgery that nicked his spleen. I didn't know anything was wrong until he came to and asked someone to call me.

But this time, I find out from Reggie, his new roommate, that Levi's got one of his physical therapy sessions at 9 a.m. now. Reggie is in his seventies and, given his slurry speech and erratically shaved head, is likely recovering from brain surgery. He wants to chat and it's a bit heartbreaking, but I couldn't give a shit. I pick up the phone on the nightstand to call Levi's mother.

"Can I talk to him?" she asks, as if *I* hadn't called *her*.

"No," I say, using a ballpoint pen to drill an angry dot into the nightstand. "He's not here. Did you know his schedule changed?"

"Oh, yes, they told me yesterday," she says. "Shall I tell him you stopped by?" In her mind, I'm like Levi's "artist phase": temporary. I tell her not to bother.

The elementary school sits right off Jamaica Avenue, a road canopied by elevated train tracks. Everything's cast in loud, grubby shadow. It's a wonder that any of my little asthmatic friends can even climb the stairs. The few bodegas around here that carry fruit and vegetables keep them in barrels outside the door—the thought of them getting near a small child's lips! It's a bad day when the state of the neighborhood's produce does me in.

For class today, I bring a striking photograph of a West African man with a pattern carved into his cheeks. "This is called scarification," I tell them. "Why might someone take part in this practice?"

"Maybe he fought a bear."

"Maybe those are tally marks—he's keeping track of something."

"Maybe that's what his father looked like, and his father."

"Maybe his wife did something bad, and he wanted to show her how much she hurt him, so he cut his face in front of her."

Maybe I won't use that picture again.

Levi apologizes for missing me in the morning.

"You better not have missed me just this morning," I say. "You better miss me every moment we're apart."

"I actually have a new partner now," he says. "I believe you've met Reggie?"

His roommate is half propped up in bed, snoring, a napkin tucked into his shirt.

"I miss you so much," I say.

"I'm right here," he says. He's not looking at me, but at the random letters he's been scrawling on his yellowing cast: *L, S, A.* He believes his feelings and compliments go without saying. He doesn't understand that I need to hear things spoken. Will I ever get to complain about something like that again? Am I ever going to get to be anything but grateful?

I add another *S* and an *A* to his doodle. "Salsa," I say. "Are you hungry?"

He shrugs. "By the way," he says, "my parents have been talking to the lawyer. He seems really smart."

Levi's decided to press charges. At first, he felt the fact that he survived was reward enough, but that was before these brutal weeks of rehab. His parents pushed for the lawsuit, but I feel that the best expenditure of everyone's energy would be to invent a time machine to stop the accident from having happened at all.

He was riding his bike when his wheel caught on a stray cement slab from a condo going up nearby. His helmet did its job, and his face was unscathed. But the truck that hit him as he plummeted toward the street did a number on everything else. One shattered shoulder, an elbow, too, bruised ribs, and, of course, his legs.

Rewind: The truck switches lanes, the construction company disposes of its materials in the appropriate manner, the city installs better bike lanes. Or Levi just takes the train that day. Problem solved.

"Who keeps texting you?" Levi asks.

I stuff my phone into my pocket. I hadn't realized it had been lighting up on the bedside table. Rico always was persistent. Levi's probably seen his name on the screen; I should probably give up.

It's not that Levi and I were ever perfect together. We fought all the time. But what were the stakes back then? There was time to improve; everything was plastic. I always imagined us morphing into something better.

"So tomorrow morning," I say, "should I not worry about coming?"

Levi sighs. "It's not like I was the one who changed the appointment time."

"If that person were here right now," I say, "the person who did change the time, I would take this knife"—I pick up a plastic knife from Levi's discarded hospital tray—"and I would slash my face to show them how much they'd hurt me." I draw the knife across my cheek hard enough to leave a scratch.

Levi says, "Not. Funny."

I'm working on a series of time-lapse drawings of rotting fruit. Weeks ago, I brought home a bagful of apples, bananas, peppers, and limes from the bodega by work. Levi complained about the flies, so I bought flypaper. Then I started making the drawings right on the flypaper. Without him here, I can use whatever paper I want, but I stick with it. There is a dark pool around the disintegrating fruit now, as if it's losing blood. The apartment smells like bad wine, which gets me in the mood, so I crack open a bottle. I get through only half a glass before there's a phone call from Levi's mother.

"If he's worrying about your feelings, Tess," she says, "it's going to take him that much longer to recover."

I try to understand what is happening. I chug my wine. It sounds like Levi's mother is dumping me.

"He needs to focus on himself for a while," she says. "He needs a break." It is all euphemisms and cloaked terms, but no less mortifying than if she'd told me outright: *You are making this worse.* I wonder if she offered to call me or if he asked her to.

"I'll give him a break," I say, touching the scrape on my cheek. "Okay."

On the night of Levi's accident, he was supposed to meet me after work. For weeks, he'd been immersed in this ridiculous graffiti project he was doing with a friend, where they were actually getting permission before they tagged people's buildings. He'd set out with his paint cans, wearing a hoodie pulled tight around his face, as if he needed the anonymity; he had permits. He was pulling inspiration from Pynchon, Foucault, and David Foster Wallace, footnotes and all. But whether he was missing the point of graffiti or not, he spent all of his time doing it, and I barely ever saw him. After a couple of weeks, I made us a dinner reservation and didn't give him the option to back out. I put on heels and lipstick, and at the dark, narrow restaurant, I perched on a barstool to wait. I texted once or twice, asking where he was. When I didn't hear back, I figured he'd forgotten. I thought, *He's in trouble now—in trouble with* me. The bartender asked me what I wanted. "Whatever you think I want," I said, holding his gaze. He mixed an elixir swirling with Cynar and Aperol and other lovely things. It was sweet but strong, and he mixed me another, and before long, I was having a nice time. An hour passed this way before I even thought to worry.

The morning after I speak to his mother is the first in ages I don't spend sitting in the Holland Tunnel. Suck it, Elizabeth. Was the red-headed girl's name Elizabeth?

This is what he wanted. But, of course, his wants and my wants are hard to separate. When he calls a little past ten, I don't answer—if I did, I can imagine how the conversation would go. I would some-how wind up making him feel better for dumping me. I put the phone in a drawer with my old paintbrushes. I used to bind them out of human hair. One of them is red. Was Sabrina her name?

At school, it's time to start on our final projects. The students choose the occasions that will inspire their creations. Many of them are taken with the idea of celebrating a passage into adulthood—they imagine themselves, at eight years old, to be quite close. Some of them are right.

After our conversation, twenty-six balloons must be inflated roughly to the size of a child's head; they will be the molds for our papier-mâché masks. I'd envisioned the kids blowing up their own balloons, but after a few spit-soaked moments, I realize they don't have the lung capacity for it.

I instruct the kids to start sketching their masks on scrap paper, and I pass Ms. Bell a bag of balloons. "What are these for?" she asks, holding fast to the pen she was using to grade. "Rewards? I don't know if they deserve them."

I explain the process. "Paste?" she says. "In here?"

"I'll clean up," I say. "I swear."

She pulls in a student teacher from down the hall, and between the three of us, we get the balloons tied off and ready to go before the kids get too wiggly. They are mesmerized, in fact, by the sight of us—grown women—puffing out our cheeks and turning red in the face. Before Ms. Bell can remember her grading, I hand her a box of rubber gloves and a stack of smocks, and she outfits the left side of the room while I tackle the right. I give them each laminated mats to cover their desks, apportioned and rubber-banded stacks of papier-mâché strips, and a small cup of water I squirt out of a jug I brought, prefilled, from home.

"You are prepared," she says.

"I'm a professional," I say. I blow up one more balloon and hand it to her.

Because I had so many supplies to carry in to work, I splurged on one of the closer metered parking spots under the elevated train. When I return after class, the car's covered in a hundred bursts of crap from the pigeons nesting overhead. As I survey the damage, a passerby remarks, "You got shit on, baby."

"No shit," I say.

"You shouldn't park your car there," he says.

"I had to carry some stuff to the school," I say. "It's the closest spot."

"You have a kid there?" he asks, nodding toward the building down the road.

I hesitate. "Yeah."

"My cousin owns a car wash a couple blocks away." His head is shaved and shiny, just like his eyes. They practically gleam.

"You've got nice eyes," I tell him.

"Let me give the compliments here," he says.

That's when I notice we're standing in front of a pet store. The window is all fogged up, and the vinyl letters on the sign are tattered and peeling. "Excuse me," I say and let myself inside through the splintering door. He follows me. He's wearing huge brown sweatpants and a matching zip-up hoodie; I imagine what it would feel like to be folded up in his arms. I want him to squeeze me to his chest, tight, until I can't breathe.

"What are you going to buy?" he asks.

"A fish," I say.

"Looks like that's about all they've got anyway," he says. "Me, I've got a dog. What do you want with a fish?"

The tank is dull and overcrowded—nothing like the one at the rehab center. "My boyfriend is in rehab," I say. "And I've gotten attached to the fish there."

"Rehab is rough," he says. "Was it court-ordered?"

The fish I want is small and orange, with diaphanous fins and a determined look on its face. I like the way it zigzags across the tank, skirting other fish, like it's got somewhere to go. "Yes," I say. "He has some issues. Vandalism, for one."

He jerks his head to the side. "You need a shoulder to cry on?"

"Do I look like I'm crying?" I ask.

The clerk scoops my fish into a tiny bowl. She pops a couple of containers of food into a bag and charges me eight dollars. I start to pull out my wallet, but the man is faster. "I got this," he says. "You live in the neighborhood?"

"More or less," I say.

"Well, I'm Andre," he says. "You come find me if it doesn't work out. If he gets put away next time. And go see my cousin." He pulls a flyer for the car wash from a plastic bag full of them. "Get that car cleaned up."

I maneuver into the apartment carrying my extra art supplies, junk mail, house keys, and the fish bowl, which I'd balanced on my lap the whole way home. As I bump the door closed with my hip, I am confronted with a veritable swarm of flies. I start to flail my arms, and I lose my grip on everything. The bowl hits the ground, the water sloshes up and out, and the fish rides the wave. The apartment isn't large, but try as I might, I cannot figure out where it went.

While I am ruining things, I dig my phone out of the drawer. I click through to one of Rico's last 2 a.m. texts—*bed is cold but u r hot*—and send him my address before getting in the shower.

When the buzzer sounds, I meet him at the door. I don't look very nice, my hair wet and stringy, and I haven't even gotten rid of all the flies, but still, we're barely inside before he has me up against the wall. I keep my head at an angle; I don't want him to kiss me, not even on the cheek.

"I thought you were never going to write back," he says, his hand under my skirt.

"I wasn't going to," I say. He has a beard now and a very small paunch above his belt. If I couldn't feel it against my own belly, I wouldn't know it was there.

"Have you been drinking?" he asks, sniffing.

"That's just the art," I say. I lift my chin over his shoulder, taking a gulp of the ferment in the air. It is hard to find the room to fill my lungs.

But the way his mouth is opening and closing on my neck makes me think of the fish. I have a vision. Somehow the fish muscled its way across the floor into the small dark space beneath the refrigerator. My knees buckle, but before I can crawl over there, I feel one of his hands on the top of my head and see the other one unzipping his pants. I let him hold me down, but I can't help it—there is something buoyant in me.

I lean back from under his grasp. "I hear my boyfriend's footsteps on the stairs."

"I don't hear anything," he says, his voice low and thick.

"You don't know what to listen for," I say, pushing him to the door.

I go into school early for my last class, armed with a box cutter to carve eyeholes into the hardened papier-mâché masks. I lose whatever extra time I built in for myself explaining to the security guard what the hell it is I think I'm doing. I rush through making my own example, gluing handfuls of feathers down at once. When the kids get started, though, the day hits a rhythm. Even Ms. Bell puts down her pen and circulates through the room as they apply paint and sundry craft materials mimicking natural resources. There are symbols, patterns, a few tears over spilled paint. One child must be stopped from licking his mask while another manages to cut off a braid and attach it to hers. If not for the school's strict no-touch policy, I'd hug them all.

I don't know why I parked in the same spot again.

Or I do know why. But when I get back to the car, there is more shit—new shit over old—and no Andre. I slump into my seat and slam the door. I miss the kids already.

I go to the car wash. I still have the flyer, and anyway, it's not too hard to find. I park and approach a cluster of guys detailing a car. They're speaking Spanish. None of them seems like a candidate for Andre's cousin. They look at me like I'm nuts. For the life of me, I don't know what I'd do with Andre if they found him for me, but I keep asking. I'm blushing and nervous, but the fact remains that my car is encrusted in pigeon shit. It has a *smell*. I head back toward it and work myself into a cold sweat trying to line up the wheels with the conveyor belts that take it through the tunnel to be cleaned. When I finally get moving, I turn off the radio and sit back, watching the water pour down around me.

I've never gotten the car washed before. It sparkles in a way I didn't remember it could. Rather than drive home, I point toward New Jersey and go.

I half expect Levi to be gone, but there he is. The bed next to him is the empty one. "You've outlasted Reggie?" I ask.

He rubs his eyes. "Am I seeing things?" he asks.

I pull out my sample mask, my Tess mask, and hold it front of my face. It looks like me, but with feathery eyebrows and a better attitude. I hold it out to him, as if it were a peace offering. He puts it on and says, "I deliberately misunderstand situations. I abandon people in the hospital for weeks at a time."

"It was only eight days," I say.

"You tell yourself that," he says.

"I started to think of you like a pot filled with water," I tell him. "That maybe you weren't boiling because I was here watching."

"Is that true?" he asks.

"If you keep that mask on," I say, "I'm only lying to myself."

He takes it off and stares at it, as if it might give him better answers. One of his casts is finally gone. I kiss him on his weak knee.

"Again," he says. "Somewhere I can feel."

I perch on the corner of his bed, about to kiss him for real. But something hard is between us, keeping us from getting close. I pull back his sheet, and there, splayed open, is a book—a fine-print study guide, liberally highlighted.

"Law school?" I ask.

He nods without meeting my eyes. His artist phase was always just temporary.

A Cane, an Anchor

Burning, the little house looks better than it ever has. Tall as the sky, its sagging roof stretches up in flames, fierce orange igniting the gray December clouds. All of our complaints—the slanted kitchen floor that makes pancakes pool at the bottom of the skillet, the shower of ceiling fragments every time a door slams—become inconsequential. More than that: We want them. We want the holes around the pipes because that's how the mice get in; we want the thin rattling windows and metronome drip of the sink. Why did we ever complain? Lou and I press against the fence, extending our fingers through the metal web toward the warmth.

Had the landlord hired professionals instead of spit-sticking all our minor tragedies back together himself, it would have been obvious that the walls weren't so much dividers of rooms as they were the trembling casings of electrical currents, thin membranes surrounding rupturing veins. "You're lucky you weren't home," everyone tells us. "We are so lucky," we say back, nodding.

But thankfulness doesn't come naturally to Lou and me. We can fake it for others just fine, but alone, we aren't expressing gratitude. What the fire didn't completely destroy, water damage finished off. The real problem, it turns out, is that even though nothing can be salvaged, we can't come up with anything besides the house that we've lost. We don't have hobbies—no half-finished knitting projects or thousand-piece puzzles. Record collections? Our music is in our phones. My jewelry, our clothes—thrift store junk. It's not like people have photo albums anymore—we don't even mourn our computer, that old thing. What have we been doing all this time?

The first few days, everything is a jumble of insurance policies and police reports and putting in for time off work. The bakery gives me leave with a shrug. Turns out I was correct in thinking my job didn't come with provisions for this kind of thing. Lou's school calls in a substitute and sends an extravagant gift basket we have to pick up at the post office. We eat chocolate-covered pretzels while sitting in our car, facing the site of our former home, neither of us motivated to pick through the detritus. We chew on leathery dried apricots as we scout a couple of dreadful short-term rentals we can't afford. I suck on a lemon drop as Lou tells me I probably left the stove on while baking, and I say he should have done something that one time he thought he smelled a strange odor emanating from the fuse box. In truth, we were Christmas shopping together when the fire broke out. Nothing but faulty wiring is to blame.

We move in with Lou's parents across town. We aren't the only refugees there. Lou's parents have taken in his uncle, Jim, whom everyone describes as "eccentric." The first few times I met him, I assumed that was a euphemism for "gay." But Lou's parents dropped in on him in New Hampshire a couple of months ago and discovered him hunkered down in a dark, unheated room, living off canned goods. Jim had vague plans to move when the time was right but apparently didn't put up much of a fight when they coaxed him out of his bunker.

As we all sit down to our first dinner together, Jim approaches the table dragging a heavy brass lamp. It has a lozenge-shaped head, a fluted stalk, and a circular base. He hauls it around with him from room to room, day and night, its cord looped and knotted. When he's stationary, he plugs it in. His assertion is that after living in low light for so long, the soft glow of this particular lamp soothes his straining eyes. I've been told not to mention it.

Over pasta and salad, Mary stares at Lou, her elbows on the table, head propped up on her hands. She has his dark, serious eyes, framed with neat plucked brows. She barely eats. "I just keep thinking, what if it had happened while you and Iris were sleeping," she says.

"Ma, like I've said . . ." Lou pauses, gesturing toward me. I chew a piece of lettuce, wondering how many days before it's appropriate to suggest arugula rather than iceberg.

"We're very lucky," I fill in. I try out an experimental smile on Lou. He returns it with irony. Luck is our shared joke.

Cast in the glow of his lamp, Jim says, "At least you have each other."

It's tempting to say that I dream of the fire, but it's not so unconscious as that. When I'm lying in bed, before I fall asleep, while I can't, I conjure it. I want to feel the shock, the jolt, the desperation again. I want it to be present tense. Now it's nothing but residuals, the headache after the flash. I close my eyes and wish back the heat.

Lou and I met at a nonprofit, where he researched grant opportunities and I struggled with Excel. We both lasted long enough to see a board member arrested for embezzling and to learn what "furlough" means. We had so much in common: the exact same coffee order, an abiding love of David Byrne, and twin mean streaks that made laughing at our coworkers' earnestness like foreplay. We were only children. Once, we ran into each other on the bus both reading Hemingway's "In Another Country" in dog-eared paperbacks of *Nick Adams Stories*. I weighed 110 pounds with my heels on and still had taut, luminous skin. He played the guitar and had large calloused hands. There were blank spaces in front of us where the rest of our lives were going to be. Had I met any other twentysomething at that office, I may well have ended up married to him.

It's strange how knowing that doesn't really matter. It was Lou then and still is.

I shift beneath the heavy crocheted blanket we're under—it reminds me of the lead drape at the dentist's—and run my nails up Lou's back. Sometimes, when he's turned away from me, I worry that I don't remember his face right. I climb over him and balance on the lip of the bed, a twin, so that we're pressed front to front. As soon as I see it, of course, I remember. His face is long, large-nosed, dark-circled, and strange. It's a face that shouldn't work but does, and not just because I love him. He has plenty of single coworkers calling, offering up their couches, their homes for the holidays. I start to feel overheated.

"I feel so close to you," he says. I keep my eyes closed so I can't confirm his sarcasm. I decide to take him at his word.

"I love you," I say. "I'm glad you didn't die in the fire."

"I was thinking about Jim," he says.

"Are you glad I didn't die?" I ask.

"Iris, Jesus. Yes," he says. "I was thinking that the lamp thing is maybe not that weird."

"The thing with his eyes," I say. "I guess it makes sense."

"No," he says. "I think it's from his old house. It might be the only thing he brought with him."

"You mean that we're the weird ones," I say. "For not having saved anything."

"For not caring," he says. I think he is going to say more, but soon his breathing evens out.

"I thought of something," I say to keep him awake. "The clock you bought me. We lost the clock."

"I didn't really buy that for you," he says. "I took it from the teacher's lounge at school. It didn't work, so no one noticed it was missing."

"Always one fifty-two. It was beautiful, though," I say. "Wasn't it? That little stopped clock with the black hands and those simple gold numbers."

"I didn't realize you really liked that thing," he says, and in a minute, he's asleep.

In the morning, we hear the lamp dragging down the hall beyond our door. Six a.m. would be sleeping in on a normal day, when Lou's teaching and I'm heading out to the bakery, but now it feels like a cruel hour. I tell Lou to put the pillow over his head, and I wiggle loose from the sheets. Clutching Mary's old bathrobe around me, I step into the dim house.

"Jim?" I whisper.

He's already dressed and dapper in a sweater vest and khakis, towing the lamp, as always. It functions as both a cane and an anchor, helping and hindering in equal measure. He looks at me with heavy eyes and says, "Good morning, sweetheart."

They continue down the hall, Jim and the lamp, looking like companions to me now. I can't bring myself to say anything. The lamp's big brass head hangs as if on stooped shoulders, tired, too.

We moved to Lou's hometown, Poughkeepsie, four years ago. After our nonprofit debacle, he decided he wanted to "give back" to his own community by teaching middle school. At a loss, I enrolled in the nearby Culinary Institute of America. I like to say I was once in the CIA. Since arriving here, we've spent Christmases with my family down in Virginia—it only seemed fair, given that we get to see his on a regular basis. But there's no way we can make the trip this year. So Lou and I sit behind his closed bedroom door and divvy up the gifts we'd purchased, deciding what to return, what to keep for ourselves, and what to repurpose as if it had been meant for his family all along. The strange outcome of having been Christmas shopping when the fire started is that we'd wound up owning only what would soon belong to others.

"Keep the scarf we got for my stepfather," I say. "Or keep it until you see if you get one better from someone else." He tucks the plaid swath of fabric behind him in the "keep" pile.

"You keep the gloves for your grandma," he says, holding out these tiny ladylike things.

"Can I pull these off?" I ask, slipping my hand into one, presenting it as if to be kissed.

He shrugs. "They're gloves."

I almost mention that he used to talk about, of all things, how beautiful my fingernails were, how their oval shape looks long and elegant even when they're cut to the quick. Bringing it up would seem like an accusation, though, which is what it probably is.

The knock on the door startles us in such a base way—we're married, thirty years old, yet suddenly, at a parent's rap on a bedroom door, we are sixteen again, scooting apart, smoothing our hair. I pull the afghan off the bed and throw it over the gifts. "Come in," I say, my voice cracking.

"You two ready?" Roy asks. He's wearing a black T-shirt and olive corduroys, faded at the knees and tight across the hips. He must have had them the first time around and continued to wear them until here they are, cool again. With his academic scruff—he teaches computer science at Vassar—and the work boots he wears to shovel snow, he's got a better, hipper look going on than either me or Lou.

"Dad," Lou says, "I really don't think we are."

"You've got to get back on the horse," he says. "You know, in the saddle."

"Who in their right mind would be showing a rental two days before Christmas?" Lou asks.

"That's why you look, son," he says. "I'm not saying move in somewhere today. I'm saying I've got a list of a few places."

"What you've got in your hand is a list of slums and crazy people," Lou says.

"I'll go," I say.

"Iris," Lou says. "I really don't want to."

"You stay here," I say. "Wrap the gifts."

It's not that I don't think Lou is right, but while Roy hasn't been acting anything but glad we're around, I can imagine we'll weigh on him before long. I see the way his eyes narrow at some of Jim's quirks—the lines the lamp scuffs on the floor, the long pauses he leaves between thoughts—and we're higher maintenance than Jim is. Our welcome will wear out. I'd like to give Roy the sense that we won't be mooching off of him forever. Unlike my parents, who split only a couple of years after they married, Roy and Mary have had a good, really normal thing going for more than thirty-five years. I've heard that kids of parents who stay together are less likely to get divorced themselves. I don't know where that leaves us.

We don't get out of the car at the first place we pull up to. "Oh, Jesus," Roy says. "This does not look like the Internet listing."

The block is in Poughkeepsie proper, not the more secluded Arlington area where Roy and Mary live. It is cartoonishly sketchy—a row of buildings leaning on each other for support, their vinyl siding scuffed with soot and their windows foggy, as if filmed with years of cooking grease. There is even a man passed out on a stoop, shoeless, his feet wrapped in bandages.

"No, let's check it out," I say. I can actually picture us living here. "I'll take a look. Which one is it?"

"Iris," he says, "I know you're an adult, but I'm going to put my foot down."

The next apartment is on the top floor of a surprisingly lovely home one town over, in Wappingers Falls. Roy exhales and says, "This is more like it." I follow him up a slate path to the front porch, climb the pleasantly creaky wooden stairs, and admire the Christmas lights wound around the slats of the railing as Roy knocks on the door.

A beautiful young woman answers and introduces herself as Ellen, the homeowner. She guides us up to the second floor. The sweet smell of a curry on the stove wafts around us, and Ellen's long hair shines under the chandelier she flicks on when we enter the apartment. After giving us an overview, she says, "I'll leave you two to look around," and winks. I get the feeling she thinks that Roy and I are a couple. I cast a quick mortified look at Roy, who is inspecting the crown molding and smiling to himself. He seems oblivious to anything but the charm of the place, which is immense. I wander through the large freshly painted bedroom to the white tiled bathroom—no stains in sight—to the kitchen, where I stand opening and closing the brand-new oven.

"What do you think?" Roy calls to me. I catch sight of him in the bedroom, giving an approving knock on the wall. He raises his eyebrows. Why is he knocking on the wall? He knows about the structure of things, about scaffolding a life so it will last. I can't help indulging the thought of living here. Of living here with Roy and not Lou. He knows so much that I don't.

"I love it," I tell him honestly.

In the car, Roy is elated, enumerating the apartment's best features. He wants to swing by the house, get Lou, sign the lease. It all seems very fast.

"Do you think we can do some errands first?" I ask.

"What do you have in mind?"

I run through a list of what I need in my head—underwear, toiletries, replacement birth control pills, a cell phone charger. Errands that, for the most part, I should keep to myself. "My paycheck is at work," I say. The bakery is just a short drive away. "They didn't know where to send it."

"We can go get it," he says. "Sure."

I crack open the SUV's window and let the winter air at my scalp. "Thanks," I say. "Although I've really enjoyed not being there. I mean, I could wait until I have to go back next week."

"Which way do you want it?" he says.

"I wish the bakery had burned down instead," I say. "Right? They're the ones with the ovens."

"Think about what you're saying." When he offers this advice, he means it. The bakery was my first job out of culinary school—I'd been so excited about the owners, Melinda and Jess, fellow CIA grads, with their technical skills, crazy flavors, tattoos, that I'd accepted bad hours and worse pay. I've learned plenty from them, but their attitudes have started to needle. It isn't just that they never thank me for the extra hours I spend perfecting their recipes. It's because they smirk when I'm kind to people. Our customers—a mix of college students and slightly confused locals—need to be welcomed and nurtured, I think. But Melinda and Jess act as if the patrons should thank us for the opportunity to have their minds blown by a piece of buckwheat black-garlic shortbread.

Lou brings home stories of discovering a student made it to seventh grade without learning to read—and then he *teaches the kid to read*. I bring home stories of Melinda insisting in front of the whole store that a gray hair found in the pinecone cupcake icing—the same icing I'd recently suggested might not actually be edible—must be mine. She and Jess had been no more than mildly concerned about my welfare postfire, willing to grant me extra days off only because they had a few aspiring-baker interns working over the holidays. They were saving money because of my personal misfortune.

"Actually, let's go there," I say. "I think I'd like to have a talk with them."

I can understand why Lou's upset. I left the house on an errand with his father and returned with no job, leaving him the sole breadwinner in this economy, in this marriage already besieged by bad luck. What I can't understand is why he's laughing so hard.

"Why is this funny?" I ask. He's still on the floor in the bedroom. His gift-sorting progress has been minimal at best. I would bet anything he'd been on the phone with one of his coworkers, one of those perky teachers with their union cards and holiday parties. I wish his phone had burned up in the fire.

"You tell me why," he says. "You think about it."

Lou, I can't help noticing, is not asking me to think for my own good. That old cliché about the apple and the tree doesn't apply to him.

"Did you, like, set our house on fire? Is that it?" He wipes his eyes.

"Are you saying I sabotage things?" I look around for a cat to hold. I wish Lou's parents had a cat I could cuddle. I wish we had a baby I could clutch to my chest, something warm and comforting.

"You know, I thought you might be proud," I say. I hang my head. In the absence of something to hold, I aim, instead, to be held. "I'm sorry."

He doesn't bite. He doesn't hold. He doesn't do what he's told; he doesn't like to be led. "Sure," he says.

Slouching out of the room, I fully intend to curl up on the couch and never get up again, but when I see Mary and Jim sitting there, cozy, enjoying the cold day off and watching a game show on TV, I find myself asking them if they'd like to have a cake. "I can whip something up, if you don't mind letting me loose in the kitchen," I say.

"If you don't mind a fat uncle," Jim says. The lamp shines a buttery glow on their faces. It's plugged in behind the couch.

"Be my guest," Mary says.

"I am," I say soberly.

The kitchen has warm seventies tiling, cavernous cabinets, and plenty of counter space. The crowning touch is a beautiful yellow KitchenAid mixer. I decide to bake a dark, spicy cake, dense and heavy enough to need a dollop of whipped cream to help it go down. In the absence of all the ingredients I'd need to make just what I want, I substitute what I find in Mary's pantry—maple syrup and brown sugar for molasses; double the cinnamon instead of nutmeg and all-spice. For all my loving feelings toward the mixer, I don't use it—beating the batter with a wooden spoon and my own bakery-strong arm feels too good. I would stir for hours if overbeating weren't a rookie mistake. Baking a cake out of spite—there's got to be a long house-wifely tradition of this.

I'm hoisting the hefty Bundt pan and batter into the oven when Lou says from behind me, "Irony?"

"I'm my own boss now," I say, brushing flour from my pants.

"Is that the plan, then?"

Oven closed, my hands empty, I'm unmoored.

"I thought of something while you were out," he says. "All of those cookbooks I bought you."

I'd only ever pretended to use them. I don't believe in cookbooks. I believe in learning a few basics and winging it from there. I know I'd mentioned that to Lou—at first I'd taken the gifts as an affront, as if he couldn't believe my own mind was better than what these experts had to offer. But then I realized it was just a failure of imagi-nation. He thought he was being thoughtful—I was a baker now, so he'd get me cookbooks. That it was actually thoughtless would have been cruel to point out. "This recipe, Lou," I lie, "it's from one of those books. I memorized it."

Hearing this, he looks happy.

We eat the cake in one sitting—before dinner, at that. We gather around the dining room table, Jim's lamp plugged in behind him, the shade angled up at the ceiling so we're illuminated by the bouncing light. The effect is beatific.

I cut thick slices for everyone, topping them with cream whipped only until it barely holds its shape. The cake is deep and sticky. I feel everyone start to love me more as they eat it.

"Those people were crazy to fire you," Jim says.

Of course, truly, nothing is forgiven. Mary's mouth tightens when we're all too stuffed to eat the roast she's made for dinner, Jim is grumpy that no one wants to join him for a game of cards, and Roy's movie choices all get shot down. "Who the hell wants to watch *Letters from Iwo Jima*," Mary says to him.

"I thought of something, Lou," I say, perching on the edge of his chair as he clicks through television channels. It's the only way I can think to get him to look away from the screen. With his eyes finally on me, I freeze up. I start to laugh. "I was going to say 'our letters.' All of our love letters burned up."

"What love letters?" he asks.

I thought he'd know I was trying to be mean. Since he doesn't, it means I really am.

He turns back to the television. I look around for another place to sit and see that everyone had been listening. They look at their hands. I stare at the television screen, thinking of that line from "In Another Country," the story we were both reading that time. It goes something like, "The war was still happening, but we didn't go to it anymore." I don't know when we stopped showing up, Lou and I, but the fire wasn't our first battle, it wasn't our last—I think, it happened after the fact.

"I'm going to go for a walk," I say.

"Me too," Jim says. I can't tell if he means to come with me or go on his own. It's been dark for hours, and now a light, dry snow has started. I pull my coat from the closet and zip myself up to the top. Mary's finger is extended as if she's going to shake it at us—she clearly wants to shut the operation down, but Roy puts his hand on her leg.

I open the front door, and the cold explodes in. "Jim?" I ask. "Shall we?" There is a moment of prayer among us while he looks between the door and the lamp. He leaves it and walks out with me.

It is miserable outside. My boots having gone up in the fire, I'm making do with sneakers. Jim takes my arm and places it in his as we start around the block. "I never thought that Poughkeepsie was pretty," he says.

"It can be," I say as we pass an old house with orange lamps burning by the doors and scalloped trim. The snow glitters in our eyelashes. "My mom was surprised I stayed here instead of going back to New York after school. But there are some nice places, cool industrial areas, Little Italy. And Lou loves his job. It's not a bad place to live."

"I used to live in New York City," Jim says. "When I was a young man."

"Did you like it?"

"It was a good place to be, you know, for people like me," he says. "Or it seemed like it anyway."

"So why did you leave for New Hampshire?"

"A man, of course," he says.

As long as Lou and I have been together, I haven't heard anything about this. "Who was he?" I ask.

"Who was he? Well, he came from a very glamorous background. By the time we met, he wasn't in touch with his family anymore, but he still had the inheritance. He never had to work but didn't look down at the people who did. I saw him around for a while—always smoking menthols, smelling sweet—before we were finally introduced, and then that was that." He pauses as we choose a direction to turn. "After we were together for a few months, maybe a year, I started to find out about these fears he had. They overwhelmed him sometimes."

I want to ask for more detail, but I hesitate. I haven't had a conversation, a real intimate conversation, with someone in a long time. "What was he afraid of?"

"It's hard to say. I'm not sure he knew. It was a real spiral. I didn't think much of it when he started refusing to go uptown—I had no use for uptown either. But then it was leaving our apartment. Then it was New York. He'd have these dreams about skyscrapers falling like dominos. He became convinced that if something was going to happen, it would happen there."

"What did you think?" I ask.

"I loved New York, but he was my world," Jim says. "It's not that it wasn't hard for me. I felt safer in New York than I ever had growing up. But I got caught up in it. When he wanted to move to this cabin, this secluded place, and he wanted to do it with me—well, gosh."

"It's romantic," I say.

"If you'd seen the canned goods, you would think otherwise," he says. "Oh, and the guns. What he thought we'd do with the guns, I can't tell you. It was the whole nine." Jim brushes his hair to the side, fixing his part.

"You certainly don't look like a survivalist," I say.

"I'd take these trips into town to buy my polo shirts and vests and loafers. He'd give me a hard time about it, but honestly, he liked the way I looked. He was sweet that way. He would just stare at me sometimes. I always knew that he loved me. As strange as our situation was, I always knew that."

Listening to him, I'd forgotten the cold. The wind breaks into his story, and I shiver, cupping my hands around my nose and mouth.

"And then what?" I ask.

"He died, of course. He was always careful that I didn't get sick, too, although sometimes I wanted nothing more than to be in it with him. That must sound crazy to you."

"No," I say, and it doesn't, although all I can think about is how, as our fire raged and died, Lou and I had extended our hands toward the heat of our burning nothings rather than toward each other.

Jim pulls me to his side. "I think it was easier for him to believe the scariest stuff was on the outside."

"Would you ever go back to New York?" I ask.

"I'm sure it's changed so much," he says.

"So have you."

"I do think about it," he says as we round the corner back toward the house.

"This is a weird question," I say. "But did he live to see September eleventh?"

Jim squeezes my arm. "Is it wrong to say that I wish he had?"

When we return, Roy and Mary have already retired. I can hear rustling upstairs, and I picture them wrapping gifts behind their closed bedroom door, as if they still have to pretend about Santa Claus. Lou is slouching on the couch, one hand in the waistband of his sweatpants, his head lolling on his shoulder. He rouses when we come in, the draft from the door ruffling his hair.

"Nice walk?" he asks.

"It was," I say, looking over at Jim. I try not to let my smile fade when I see that he's by the lamp, a sliver of pale skin exposed below his shirt as he reaches to unplug it.

He stands up with effort and says, "Good night, you two." I wish he would stay and talk to us, talk to us all night, but he gives us a salute and drags the lamp up to his room.

I sit sideways on the couch facing Lou, tucking my cold toes beneath his thigh. I take a corduroy blanket from the armrest behind me and pull it up to my eyes. "Do you want to go see that apartment tomorrow?" I ask.

He looks down at his cuticles. "You don't want that apartment," he says.

"It was beautiful," I tell him.

"It was so beautiful you quit your job, is that it?" he says, then sighs. "Look, I don't want to fight."

"What if I do?" I ask, dropping the blanket from around me. "What if I do want to fight?"

I reach for him. Hands poised in front of me, I throw my weight at his thin chest. The blow makes a hollow sound as it lands, and he blinks, stunned. I grab his shoulder, and instead of pushing again, I pull him toward me so that his face is right up close to mine, so that his eyes and mine are matched and we're breathing each other's breath. "I want to fight," I say.

LOCAL NEWS

Even though the sound of the crash jolts me from sleep, I still think it must have been a dream—I relegate it to that other world. Only when the beam of a flashlight slices through my window do I sit up in bed and peer outside

There is a car bisected by a lamppost. The light is out, the street dark but for the flashing red and blue of the police cars. I'm glad I didn't see the crash. There are two female and two male officers. One has the driver pinned under his knee. He's skinny, probably just a kid. His leg splays at an odd angle as they cuff him, and he cries as they bend back his arms.

"I see you," I hear a voice call. "I see you and I'm recording this."

It's my upstairs neighbor, Ellis. The flashlight illuminates a path from the street to his window. No one is impressed. They hoist the kid to his feet, but the one leg buckles beneath him. He yelps, keels sideways. They drag him down the street.

Only in New York, I think, pulling the sheet to my chin and hoping for sleep. I should be at work in four hours. But only ten minutes later, I'm buttoning a cardigan and walking up to the fourth floor.

"Was that police brutality?" I ask.

Ellis tugs down his T-shirt in the back—he must have just pulled it on when he heard the knock at his door—and steps aside to let me in. "I'm primed to see the worst," he says. "You know the councilman I work for? He's the one that got detained during the West Indian Day Parade last year. The cops didn't believe that a big black guy could be an elected official."

"I didn't know you worked in government," I say. When I see Ellis, usually it's after work, sitting on our stoop, talking about a few TV shows we both like or what we're going to make for dinner. What did I think he did? He's usually in a suit, so I assumed something I'd be bored by. His apartment smells like sleep, stuffy and airless, but also like coffee. The layout is the same as mine, so when Ellis gestures toward the kitchen, I lead the way.

He offers me coffee, but I'm not sure about having a cup at five in the morning. I contemplate for long enough that he just pours for himself. The floor is the same cheap black-flecked linoleum as mine, but cleaner. The black flecks, in my mind, make it look perpetually dirty, so I rarely bother to sweep. There are dishes in the drainer beside his sink, two wineglasses upturned on the top rack.

"Should we send your video to the news?" I ask.

"Oh, that," he says, scratching the stubble darkening his jawline. "I was so amped up, in the moment, that I couldn't find my phone."

"You lied?"

"Didn't do much good," he says, leaning up against the counter. "That kid's leg is never going to be the same. Did you see them shoving him into the patrol car? What he needed was an ambulance."

I see Ellis's gaze flit to my chest, then back up to my face. I can't believe I came up here without putting on a bra. "I feel like the person with the microphone in her face," I say. "The one insisting, 'But this is usually such a quiet neighborhood.'"

"Is it, though?" he asks, then takes a breath. "You know what? I think it's a little too early to have that whole conversation." I exhale. He pours me a mug of coffee and says, "One for the road."

Hours later, at work, I tell Andrea about my morning. We're paging through wedding blogs, trolling for photos that feature our floral designs. She's stuck on the Ellis part.

"So, he's in politics?" she asks. "That means he's ambitious."

"I'm not going to date a neighbor, if that's what you're thinking," I say. "That could get really messy."

"Of course not," she says. "But what if you fixed me up?"

Working in the wedding industry, as florists do, can make a person lean in one of a few directions. Andrea wants nothing more than to meet a nice eligible man and hit all the marks: first date, key exchange, big white dress, honeymoon on the beach. And I want all the suckers out there to want what she wants so I can keep getting paid.

"I think he's dating someone," I tell her. "I saw two wineglasses drying on his dish rack."

"So you *are* interested," she says, smoothing her bangs across her forehead, a haughty downturn to her mouth.

"That wasn't actually the gist of my story," I say, right-clicking to copy a photo of a glorious bright yellow arrangement we'd made last spring. "To me, the most salient part was the injured teen being hauled off by police officers."

"I get it," she says. "I'm a bad person. I've got some sick priorities."

She ducks her head in this way she does, hiding behind her hand. When we were introduced by a former boss, I never thought this would work, but Andrea's got an eye for business as much as she does for flowers; she's good at all the aspects of the job I'm not. We work as a unit, in a state of pure symbiosis. She's already loaded half the photos we found into a new portfolio on our website.

"You're not a bad person," I say. "I'll ask Ellis if he's seeing anyone."

On the way home from work, I take a detour to pass by our neighborhood precinct. I've never been inside a police station, or even spoken to a cop. What would I say? Would I make some sort of accusation? Simply ask what happened? I have a feeling that what I saw probably wasn't that unusual. I buy a six-pack at the bodega and head home.

I'm in our vestibule transferring the beer into a thermos when Ellis rounds the corner. "Can you ask your councilperson to do something about these open-container laws?" I ask, emerging onto the stoop. "Beer tastes so much better when you can drink it in public."

"I'm on it," he says, hitching up his pants to join me on the top step. I offer him the thermos, and he takes a gulp. Gesturing at the scene in front of us—sparkling windshield confetti still on the street, the busted lamp cordoned off by yellow crime-scene tape—he adds, "I filed a complaint about this. Lot of good it will do, but at least it's on the record."

"I stood in front of the police precinct for four or five minutes," I say. "So that was my contribution."

"Hurting the cause," he says.

"How do you mean?" I ask, shifting uncomfortably on the step, its sandpaper texture pilling my skirt.

"You gave them something nice to look at," he says, punching me on the arm. He's your neighbor, I remind myself, willing the tingles away.

"How do you feel about setups?" I ask.

He leans back on his elbows and looks up at the dusk sky. "It all depends," he says.

"I was telling my coworker about this morning, and she was curious about you," I say. "She's single. She'd love to get a drink."

He tilts his head, finishing the last of the beer in my thermos. "Speaking of drinks," he says, "we're out."

I tuck the empty thermos into my purse. We sidestep the broken glass and walk the couple of blocks to our neighborhood bar. It's got deep leather banquettes and a giant window overlooking the street. Ellis buys me a Sixpoint. "It's like what you were drinking on the stoop," he says, wielding an amber pint. "I hope you don't mind that I ordered for you."

"I would, usually," I say, taking a sip. "But you got it right."

He has a scotch in his hand, and slides in next to me in the corner booth I've chosen. He finishes half his drink in one swallow.

"About that setup," I say.

"I'm kind of seeing someone," he says. "But it's casual."

"So you'd be open to it." I don't know why I'm pressing. I don't think he would even like Andrea, nor she him. I watch his throat as he swallows his scotch, the way it contracts and relaxes like a heart beating.

When I finish my beer, he gets both of us another. He tells me about his work, what it's like interfacing with the neighborhood's old guard in their church meeting rooms and the new families at the food co-op. "Sometimes, I'm dealing with putting in a speed bump on a certain block where people drive too fast," he says. "But there's more serious stuff, too. It can be like social work. I like getting to know the kids."

"I arrange flowers," I say. "I make pretty flowers look prettier."

A drink later, we're making out in the booth like we're twenty-two, or maybe sixteen, rather than in our thirties. He has one arm circled around me, his fingers fitting into the spaces between my ribs. I couldn't pull away if I tried, but I don't try.

It's raining by the time we leave the bar to head back to our building. We hurry down the street, heads bowed. I'm not sure what's going to happen when we arrive. The scenario I want to want and the scenario I actually want are diverging. Are we going home together or just going home?

I stop short in front of my door; he's nearly across the landing before he seems to notice he should say good night. I reach into my pocket for my keys, and he leaves me on the third floor with an unsentimental parting kiss. "You can give my number to your coworker, if you want," he says as he heads upstairs.

Inside my apartment, I consider setting fire to the building. I would sacrifice all my stuff to get to his—that would teach him. The room spins. I lie down on the couch and flip on the local news. I catch the tail end of a story about a car chase. The stolen car, the one that crashed into the lamppost outside my window, belonged to a neighborhood pastor, a guy who literally used his car to deliver meals to homebound parishioners. The kid was a kid, but also wasn't—he'd just turned eighteen. "Jesus Christ," I say, looking longingly across my apartment toward a box of cookies on the kitchen counter. At this point, I would even eat the one I can see on the floor, which I must have dropped earlier. But the distance is insurmountable. I fall asleep in my clothes, smelling like a brewery, the rain relentless against my window.

The next day we have a wedding. I meet Andrea at the venue, an early nineteenth-century boardinghouse that up until a year ago was home to a maritime museum. It has a weathered brick facade, uneven floorboards, and a haunted reputation. Because a flood wiped out its basement electrical systems, it runs on generators instead of normal electricity, but the occasional power outage adds to the old-timey charm of the place. New Yorkers pay extra for that kind of thing.

I convinced the couple getting hitched—older, a second marriage for each—that they should double down on the flowers. I wanted to see what the space would look like filled to the rafters, and they agreed. We cart in huge, sprawling creations—some need to be raised through the window with a rope, since there aren't any working elevators in the building. As soon as we get them in place, I know I was right to insist on supersized arrangements. The one that sits on the mantel stretches nearly to the ceiling, with a tangle of branches and allium, a certain kind of globular flower that reminds me, in equal measure, of a dandelion puff and a crystal ball. Onions are a kind of allium, too, which gives the flowers a secret sourness, an appealing dark side. Down between the plates and lines of wineglasses on the communal dining table, we place a row of smaller, tighter bouquets so that no one's view will be blocked. Over the two sets of doors, we hang cascading garlands that will brush guests' cheeks as they enter the space. When we're done arranging everything, I am nearly in tears, it is so perfect.

"Alliums again?" Andrea asks, seeing me blinking. Her curly blond hair is piled on top of her head and held in place by two blue ballpoint pens, her weekend work 'do. "I don't know why you always insist on them when you're so clearly allergic."

"Damn alliums," I say.

I'd like to replay last night for Andrea and see if she thinks that, actually, Ellis expected me to follow him up to his place, that it was me, not him, who made the decision to end last night where it ended. But even thinking about all this reminds me, once again, that getting involved with a neighbor is not the smartest thing.

In the building's dim stairwell, I hang several mason jars filled with single blooms—my last task. I listen for footsteps as I go. A hundred fifty years ago, a knife fight happened right here: a long-shoreman and a chandler, battling over the love of an Irish domestic who lived in the attic. Somehow, she, too, was killed in the tussle. The legend goes that she's still running down the stairs to intervene. I make it to the ground floor, however, without encountering any ghosts.

When I get to the foot of the stairs, I realize I have one extra jar. I hold it up high and release, flinching at the sharp crack of the glass against the concrete landing. In this job, I put together a dream world, and as soon as it's perfect, I leave. But this time, I want to be here longer. I start to push together glass fragments with my foot, breathing in the fragrant air.

"Tell me that was extra," Andrea says, flipping through a stapled set of paperwork.

"I got Ellis's number for you," I say as I gingerly pluck the biggest shards of glass from the floor.

"*His* number for *me*." She grimaces. "Why didn't you give him mine?"

"He probably wouldn't have called," I say. "I don't mean that in a bad way." I gather the last of the broken glass into my hand, holding it loosely so I don't cut myself, and head upstairs to find a trash can.

Andrea's already at the shop when I get there Monday. I'm carrying two coffees, hers doctored with Splenda and soy. She's at our little desk with two coffees, too, mine swirling with half-and-half and a dash of cinnamon.

"Gosh," I say, smiling.

"I would say 'Great minds think alike,'" she says. "But . . ."

I take a few swigs from one cup, then the other. "We're going to have to do a lap around the block to work off the caffeine."

"But," she repeats, "I went out with Ellis last night."

I swallow hard. "On a Sunday, huh," I say. "That's unexpected."

"Speaking of unexpected," she says, "you never told me he was black."

I spin in my chair to look at her straight on. She's red all the way up to her hairline. "It's not like I withheld the information," I say. "I didn't really tell you anything about him. You wanted to meet him based on the fact, it seemed, that I sort of liked him."

Andrea blows on her coffee. "That's essentially the opposite of what you said before."

"Whatever," I say. In a more charitable mood, I would have said that wasn't how I felt before, either. "But, anyway, it matters to you? That he's black?"

She clenches her fist on the desk, a move I usually only see when she's on the phone with a particularly difficult client. "I sat next to him at the bar, and I didn't even think to ask if he was the guy I was meeting. Because I didn't know I was meeting a black guy. *That's* why it matters. We made it through almost a whole drink sitting next to each other without putting it together. We never would have, in fact, if he didn't randomly strike up a conversation with me. I was mortified."

I do some soul-searching, as much as I can do in a few blinks. Did I not tell her for a reason? Did I want her to look stupid? It's not like Ellis and I pretend to be color-blind or something—didn't we just have a conversation about stop-and-frisk?

"Forget telling you that he's black," I say. "What I should have told you is that I made out with him the other night, and then he ditched me at my door."

Andrea finishes one of her coffees. "I know," she says.

I wait a beat to see if she expects an apology. I probably owe her one. But she reaches across our desk and puts her hand on mine.

"He told me," she says. "After we had a drink, it was clear we weren't going to hit it off. Not in that way. So we talked about you."

"Don't even tell me," I say. "I don't want to hear what he said."

"Are you sure?" she says. "Because—"

"No," I say. "I have to see this guy at the mailboxes. I shouldn't know any more about him than I do the eighty-year-old lady who lives on the first floor." I excuse myself to the bathroom.

At home, I sit on the stoop, no drink this time. I get up at one point to help Mrs. Lambert up the stairs. I know her whole life story, I have to admit. She's lived in our building since the 1950s and used to work one of the jewelry counters at Macy's until her arthritis got too bad to couple all the clasps. She's married, but her first husband, who died in Korea, was the love of her life.

"You look well," she says to me as I lift her grocery bags. "That lipstick suits you."

The door clicks behind her. I watch a swarm of middle school boys ride by on their bikes, all chaos and noise. One of them rams another one off his seat, and he splats down on the pavement. He's still for a moment before bringing his knees to his chest and kicking himself upright like an action movie star. He hoists his entire bike chest-high and throws it at the kid who knocked him over. That boy takes a handlebar to the face. His eyes fill up for a moment before he starts to laugh. They all climb back onto their rides, oblivious to the broken glass crunching under their tires.

"Don't you wish you were twelve again?" Ellis asks, coming up the sidewalk. We watch as the boys zigzag down the middle of the next block, then disappear around the corner.

"If I could be a twelve-year-old *boy*, maybe," I say.

"You're not drinking today," he observes. "I could use one, the way this week is going."

"It's only Monday," I say.

He's got his eyes closed, rubbing the bridge of his nose between his thumb and forefinger. His shirt is untucked, the top two buttons undone, and there are halos of sweat under his arms. "Tell me about it."

"I heard about your date with Andrea," I say.

"Is that what that was?"

"It wasn't my best idea," I say. "I mean, you're seeing someone."

He squints at me. "That's why you think it was a bad idea?"

In front of us, the ruins of the lamppost still block the sidewalk. I wonder if they'll stay like that forever. Upstairs, crumbs still litter my kitchen floor. I stand, dust off my jeans, and unlock our front door.

THE LAST UNICORN

Dax and I stand on either side of the volleyball net behind the supermarket. It is too early for the cohort of Central American men who frequent the court to be out playing. It is too early for anyone who doesn't have a tiny miserable child to be up on a Saturday morning. As a gesture of goodwill toward our neighbors, I've strapped ours to my chest and headed out to do some misty sunrise grocery shopping. Who knew there were so many twenty-four-hour businesses in Sunnyside, Queens?

"Meg, we should have brought a ball," Dax says.

I gesture at the just-dozing baby suspended from my shoulders in his comfortable jersey sling. "He's pretty round," I say.

Dax shakes his head. "Leaden, though. He'd never get over the net."

I root through our pile of grocery bags and extract a carton of eggs.

"We can't," he says, although his smile says otherwise. The postbaby unruliness of his beard makes him seem all the more mischievous.

I launch an egg. It explodes on my half of the court. I feel grateful that the falling rain will wash away the mess before the real players arrive. Dax boos. I try again, tossing one up and swatting at it on its descent, sending it straight forward with impressive velocity. It sails through, rather than over, the net and hits Dax just below his rib cage. He catches it before it falls, lobbing it back at me. I leap out of the way, jostling the baby.

"This, he sleeps through," I say, making sure his head is secure and supported. I attempt to dropkick another egg; it hatches goo all over my shoe.

Dax crouches, in hysterics. "Why would you do that?"

My sock starts to fill with viscous egg-guts. "Come here," I say, and the fool, he comes. When he gets close enough, I smash an egg in his hair.

I work in a small maritime museum that's in the process of failing. Its electrical systems were destroyed by a freak East Coast flood, adding several million dollars to an already impressive debt. Of course, it makes perfect sense for it to close. New York has a long history of erasing its past; it doesn't even remember enough to recognize the pattern. The most deranged part of the whole situation, though, is that no one will cop to what is about to go down any week now. Deadlines get extended, then extended again. I'm working off a generator, on text for an exhibition that's supposed to open in two months. But by then, barring divine intervention, this place will likely be a thing of the past.

"I'm going to do a universal find-and-replace," I say to Isabel, the other curatorial assistant. "I'm going to add the word 'alleged' to every sentence. *This alleged exhibition seeks to tell the alleged story . . .*"

"No one would notice," she says. "Guaranteed."

"Certainly not the visitors," I say. Isabel snorts. We haven't had "visitors," plural, in months. We're technically closed to the public, although we're not supposed to say that's a permanent state of affairs. We pretend that there are repairs going on, as if someone merely is taking a wrench to a leaky sink.

"What's Buster doing right now?" Isabel asks.

I check my watch. "He's screaming his face off, I'm sure. My mother-in-law probably is swigging white wine, trying to get him to take his bottle."

"Really?"

I shake my head. I feel guilty, of course. Most of the staff doesn't even come in to work anymore—I could smuggle the baby in with me if I wanted. When well fed, he's not the worst coworker a person could have. But my mother-in-law lives close by, and she likes me so much more now that I have him. "Let's go meditate," I say.

We head out into the empty museum galleries, all of the collection's objects having been shuttled off to a safe, dry storage facility upstate. Because our building is over two hundred years old—ancient in New York years—it's actually more interesting when stripped like this. The exposed brick is the stuff of real estate legend, the wooden ceiling beams low and lovely. There are panels of graffiti where nineteenth-century workers drew caricatures of their crazy bosses and cannons that look like penises. Isabel and I take daily breaks to sit cross-legged on the beautiful warped floorboards, out of the close stuffy air of our office cubicles.

I flatten my hands on the floor and think of the day I was hired, when I'd felt, finally, I'd figured something out. I was no longer aspiring; I was there. Ever since I knew what curators were, I'd wanted to be one. That's what I dreamed of—not a house or a wedding or a family but a job. This job. Being a curator is about vision, about telling stories, about assembling objects so people can make connections, feel ideas spark. "You know we'll never get curatorial jobs again," I say.

"I know," she says. "You think I haven't been looking? They're unicorns, jobs like this."

"We know the ghosts here so well," I say. "Just once, I want to meet one for real."

Isabel and I have spent weeks paging through the census records for the part of the museum that used to board sailors, sea captains, and longshoremen. There was a list of domestics—young Irish women who lived in the cramped quarters up above the hotel rooms and tended to the laundry and upkeep of the men downstairs. We picked upstairs-downstairs pairs at random—Erin Fitzpatrick and Joe Schaeffer, Mary Cleary and John McClanahan—conjuring the love affairs, the chance meetings in the hall, how Erin would run her fingers over Joe's name, sewn onto the collar of his shirts, how John would ply Mary with mugs of ale from the corner pub. None of the ghost stories people tell about this place are based in truth, but that doesn't mean there aren't others stories, ones we don't yet know.

"How's your Irish accent?" Isabel asks, affecting hers, which isn't bad. "We would want to blend in."

"I've seen the Irish Sea, you know," I say. "It's the most beautiful blue green. I can just imagine those girls, their stomachs bottoming out when they saw the opaque New York City water."

"It was worse back then," Isabel says. "It really used to smell."

"But I bet they were relieved to be here," I say. "When their ships docked? After all those weeks of uncertainty at sea."

"Even though there was no Brooklyn Bridge yet, no Statue of Liberty," Isabel says, "it was probably still beautiful."

"So what would we have been?" I ask. "Maids? Cooks?"

"Prostitutes? Mothers?" Isabel says. "You know, my little brother said the other day that women didn't used to work, not until the 1970s. As if life was for leisure before that."

"These women"—I sweep my arm out, embracing the Marys and the Erins who once stood where we sit, who probably never sat, not for all the hours they worked here—"were superheroes."

After the baby is bathed, sweet-smelling, and sleeping, I root through the kitchen for something to eat. Dax says, "I'll order. You can look all you want, but bare is bare."

"Didn't we just go grocery shopping?" I ask. When I moved in with Dax, I assumed our fridge would always be full; he's a butcher, after all. I worried, actually, about the temptation of a constant influx of meat. I was vegan for much of my teens and twenties; as much as I love it now, red meat does a number on my system. But Dax doesn't bring his work home with him; turns out he has to pay just the same as anyone who wants a steak from his store.

"It's been awhile," he says. "I had to throw out some of the vegetables we didn't cook in time."

"You could have mentioned that earlier," I say. "You know I get hungry after feeding your son." I narrow my eyes at him, daring him to say something about how I'm breast-feeding only before bed now.

Dax has gotten better at backing off. I watch his jaw tighten as he swallows a retort. I don't feel triumphant about the changes I've inspired in him. We've been married only a year, and already I've made a quiet man quieter.

"Who should I call?" he asks.

"Sushi," I say, kissing the tense place under his ear. "Brown rice."

"Can you have raw fish again?" he asks.

"Who cares," I say, withdrawing. "You think people used to worry about that? Our mothers or their mothers? Not a chance. I need protein." I tell myself to relax, but whose body is it? I'm still not used to being questioned, to living in such close proximity to another person's opinions. Two years ago, I'd never heard of Dax, and now here he is, my husband, father of my child, questioning my dietary choices.

He leans against the rolling cart, sending it into the side of the fridge. We'd imagined that we would rest our cutting boards on the cart, that we would still cook after Buster was born. He reaches for the phone. "I'll go shopping tomorrow," he says.

I fling my arms around his neck and hang there. I love feeling the strain of his muscles as he holds me up. I don't need an out-of-body experience to know how mercurial I can be. I can see it right from here. It's tempting to blame it on hormones or job stress, but even now, swayed by surging and retreating waves of love and

ambivalence, there isn't much truth to that. *This is who you married,*
I'm always saying. *It's not my fault you didn't know it.*

He unhooks me and orders. I watch his mouth move as he speaks
on the phone. I thought we'd have a few years to get to know each
other better before we were too tired to pursue dinner conversation,
but here we are. He has a little bit of blood on the cuff of his pants,
inevitable in his line of work. His bare toes are craggy and calloused.
It would have been so easy for us not to have met, for us to have been
two ships passing in the night. Who gets together in bars anymore?

He hangs up, and I ask, "Who the hell are you?"

"Mama," he says, opening himself a beer, "I think you need more
sleep."

Despite everything, when the day comes that I am out of work, I'm
stunned. My boss calls me into his office, and I think he's going to
chastise me for changing exhibition text without approval, which I'd
been doing freely, or for the century-old sailor's valentine I'd appro-
priated, a wooden box embellished with tiny pink shells, now full of
paper clips and rubber bands.

"But I have a baby," I say.

"I lost my job, too," he says. "We all have. You obviously knew
this could happen."

"I was used to expecting it," I say. "Worrying about failure—
that's what I do. It keeps me from failing."

"I can write you a recommendation," he says.

I know I should thank him, but instead I sit in silence. I stare at
his hairline, pinpricked with sweat. I have the overwhelming feeling
that this is my fault, that if only I'd tried a little harder, I could have
saved this place. My boss asks me to return my keys.

"This building is going to become a mall, isn't it?" I ask, breaking
a nail as I pull the keys off my key ring.

"Something like that," he says.

Isabel and I leave someone else to pack up, and we sneak out to the water, onto one of the museum's historic ships. The schooner is beautiful, its sails cutting white triangles against the skyline, but it isn't seaworthy. We can see the dark lower levels through holes in the deck beneath our feet. The river rocks us into queasiness; we crouch behind a stack of crates, and Isabel lights a cigarette.

"I heard them talking before I left yesterday," she says. "I debated calling you but thought I'd let you have a few more hours of blissful ignorance."

"Did you bust into the boardroom and demand answers?" I ask. "Did you tell them off?"

She's wearing different clothes than yesterday, but her hair is pulled into an oily ponytail and there are echoes of eyeliner beneath her lashes. A faint vertical line runs from her forehead to her chin, her foundation in place on one side of it, rubbed off on the other. Her pillow must need a good soak.

"Went to happy hour," she says. "Can't you tell? I was there until someone called me a cab."

"Bad Isabel," I say. "That's not healthy."

"You're not single," she says. "You have a safety net."

"Dax?" I ask. "That's safe?"

"You're having problems?"

"I don't think so," I say. "I'm just asking. Do you think we're safe? I can't tell. We see each other so little."

"That'll change now, huh?" she says. "I guess you'll stay home with Buster."

I shake my head. "He doesn't deserve that," I say. "I love him too much."

"I think I have to get out of New York," she says. "Learn some other city's history."

I lower myself down onto the damp, rotting deck. Isabel lies down next to me. The sky looks the same as it did a hundred years ago. If I tilted my head just to the left, I would see the Freedom Tower.

If I leaned just to the right, there would be the Brooklyn Bridge, the strings of its harp playing their singular, silent song. But looking straight up, it's just blue. I could be anywhere, anytime. It wasn't long ago that I was when and where I wanted to be—in retrospect, it was just this morning. "Let's steal this ship," I say. "We'll be rumrunners. Curse like sea captains. Get tattoos and rule the river."

"I like the sound of that," she says.

I show up midday at Dax's shop and slip in through the open door. He's elbow-deep in a carcass. It's perverse, seeing the pig he has tattooed on his arm poised over its fallen brethren. He wears a stained white apron and a backward baseball cap. The neighborhood teenager he hired to man the register is huddled over his phone, oblivious. I perch on the sill of the plate glass window. Subway tiles line the walls, lightbulbs hang on wires, and the meat cases are trimmed in chrome: simple, classic. The ceiling, through pure luck, is pressed tin. Dax doesn't follow trends in all things, but in his shop, his interests aligned with fashion in a way that telegraphed a certain level of success from the beginning. Although he's not raking it in—Buster's college fund would be nonexistent but for his grandparents—he's profiled constantly, looking handsome and holding a cleaver, in this or that magazine. He mentions sometimes, in those articles, that his wife is a curator. What will he say now?

When Dax finally notices I'm there, he reacts with such a start that I realize, not for the first time, that one shouldn't surprise a butcher at work. His knife flails dangerously close to the kid at the register. Dax sends him to the back to package some orders.

"Buster?" he asks, worried, his eyes jumping from spot to spot.

"Of course not," I say. "Your mom's got him—he's fine. I'm here looking for a job, actually. You hiring?"

"Those bastards." He looks down at his scuffed sneakers, then back up at me. "You shouldn't cry. You've hated it for so long."

I shake my head, wiping my eyes with the heel of my hand. It isn't true—I wasn't happy, sure, but is that the same as hating it? The job, as much as it eventually became about its own imminent end, gave my days shape. I knew who I was there more than I do anywhere with him, or with Buster. I've known the ghosts of that place longer than I've known either of them.

Dax lifts the gate beside the cash register, holds open an apron, and ties it at my waist, his arms folding around me as he makes the knot. Behind the counter, the mineral smell of meat fills my nose. I pull on gloves, and he shows me where to place the knife, how to press down until I hear the crack of bone. What were butchers doing a century ago? This. Separating limb from joint, muscle from fat. Feeding their neighbors and their families. I press a thumb into the pink meat, feeling the gentle give, the cool resistance.

"Want to get matching tattoos after this?" I ask.

He nods. "'Buster,' right across our necks?"

"His face on our foreheads," I counter.

"His handprints, crawling up our backs."

"His little feet," I say, picturing their warmth and weight.

Dax shows me the next cut to make. The flesh parts under my knife, easy, like it was meant to do just that.

POUGHKEEPSIE

We're on our way to the hospital, and I keep missing the turnoff. Swing back through the center of town, Claire sliding lower in the passenger seat as I take the curve too fast. Only three glasses of wine, but that was two too many. Clearly. Claire's not making any snarky comments, so this is serious. Her mouth is tight, lines fanning out beside her eyes. "I'm sorry, I'm sorry," I chant. Of course, we should have called an ambulance, but while she was still lucid, Claire begged me not to: "You know what those things cost?"

Poughkeepsie has this loop through downtown, lanes shooting off to the civic center, the train station, the high bridge across the Hudson. At one point, there's an intersection where it's supposedly legal to take a left on red. I've done it a few times, but I'm still not convinced. The hospital is just before the water. I'm panicking that I'll wind up on the bridge.

"Almost there," I say. "You hanging in? You okay?"

Damp sheen on her forehead. Losing color until, instead of white, she flashes red-blue, red-blue. Only eleven, but the road's empty. No question who's getting pulled over.

On the far side of the loop now. Veer onto the shoulder, in front of a church. Hit the curb and hear the hubcaps scrape. Lurch to a stop as a tire deflates. I roll down the window with one hand, cover my mouth with the other, sniffing to see if I can smell the wine. I can.

The officer approaches. Middle-aged, wire-framed glasses. I glance at Claire, not putting on an act when I start to cry. She looks like death. I don't wait for him to say his piece. I say, "Please help us."

Three days later, Claire's still in the hospital. I've lost my license.

"Apparently, there're no excuse for driving drunk in this town," I say, sitting on the stained chair at Claire's bedside. A strange bitter smell.

"So no chance you can go get me something to eat from Adams," she says. Her eyes are half-closed, purple smudges beneath them, and her hair is a tangled mess across her pillow.

"They're letting you eat?" I ask.

"In theory," she says, gesturing at the abandoned tray of food on the stand beside her. I hadn't noticed the other strange smell in the room was emanating from it. "But they give the same thing to everyone, no matter what they're allowed."

Claire lays it all out. The real tragedy isn't the horrible pain, but how she won't be able to eat fat anymore. The problem seems to be, of all things, her spleen. "I'm subsisting on applesauce," she says. "Oh, and my parents want me to come stay with them when I'm discharged."

I glance over my shoulder to make sure they're not behind me, even though I know they're in Colorado. Claire had me call to convince them not to fly in.

"You can't," I say. "I've been sleeping with a steak knife. A three-bedroom Victorian is great and all, until it's just you, the dark, and a lot of creepy creaking sounds."

"I guess you need sharper knives," she says. "Back in Brooklyn, we never cooked. By the way, how are you getting to work?"

"Walking," I say. "None of the bus routes come close enough."

"Pioneers," Claire says—our ironic refrain since moving here on little more than a whim, what we say instead of "This might have been a mistake."

"Pioneers," I say.

"I'm so sorry," she says, pointing at the various monitors around her. "My deductible is like five thousand dollars—after what all this is going to cost, I might as well have taken an ambulance."

I flex my calf for her. "All the walking might get me in shape, at least."

Her smile is wan, and I realize my mistake. Claire is a dancer. She's been assisting in Vassar's modern program since we arrived, and she was hoping to dazzle them enough that they'd hire her on full-time next semester.

"You'll be back at work in no time," I say.

"I'll be skinnier, at least," she says.

"I'm so sorry," I say, bending to kiss her on the cheek. "Sorrier than you. But I should go to work."

Outside the hospital, her sick smell is still in my nose. I take a few pulls of the dry November chill and check my watch. I have ten or so years on my project manager, which gives me a measure of authority. If I say I have to come in late, I do. But it's eleven now, and if I walked, I wouldn't get there until after lunch. It's the first job I've had that makes me care about things like that. I accepted it before I even heard how much it paid. Not much, it turns out, even for this town.

The hospital is one of the few places in Poughkeepsie where it's possible to flag down a cab. The others are the train station, the mall, and the Super Stop & Shop. I climb in and let the driver know where I'm headed. He adjusts the rearview mirror so he can look me in the eye. He's around my age; his shirt is buttoned all the way to the collar, and his hair is parted perfectly to the side. "Really?" he asks.

His trepidation is understandable. I work in what is essentially still an abandoned lightbulb factory. It is four stories high, nearly a block long, and took almost a year of professional labor to stabilize enough so we, the *non*professional labor, could start the next stage of renovations. But it's a dreamy place. The bricks are weathered, the windowpanes cloudy, and the metal is oxidized to the perfect shade of green. In Brooklyn, it would have been turned into condos ten years ago.

"We're fixing it up," I tell him. "Upstairs will be affordable live-work space for artists. The first floor will have a media lab for local kids, and a café, too. A whole community."

"You don't seem like a construction worker," he says.

"You don't seem like a cabdriver," I say, although really he does, with his un-American style and slight accent. I'm not sure if I sound more or less like a jerk for having said it.

He angles the mirror again. "I've been driving this cab for two years."

"And before that?"

"I was a student in Albania. My cousin brought me over here. You?"

"My roommate and I saw an interview with this musician who said that New York was great in the seventies when she was coming up, but now it hates artists. She said we should all move to Poughkeepsie if we wanted to make a go of it. We've been here three months."

He pulls up in front of the factory. "So you moved here because a pop star told you to?"

"Some people listen to their pastors, some to their parents—Claire and I listen to Patti Smith," I say.

"And Claire—she's the one in the hospital?"

"She is." I riffle through my purse for my wallet. I am five dollars short. "I'm a jackass," I tell him. "Let me find someone to borrow from."

"Can I come in with you?" he asks.

Edi and I climb to the third floor before we find anyone. "You're going to put in an elevator?" he asks. He's breathing fine; I'm the one panting.

Giovanni is crouched and wielding a hammer the size of his forearm, wrenching nails from the floorboards. His long hair is wound into a bun on top of his head, and his jeans hang low enough that we get quite a view from behind.

"Gio," I say, "can I borrow ten dollars?"

"Five," Edi says. "Five is fine." He's halfway across the room already, toeing the loose wood beams, examining the mottled windowpanes.

"Ten," I whisper to Gio.

"This guy extorting you?" he asks. He doesn't seem concerned, per se—maybe a little excited by the prospect. When I first started here, I tried to hang out with him and the rest of the gang, but they're too idealistic for me, or maybe just too young. They like to get high and wax philosophical on long walks in the woods; they like driving over the bridge to rage at New Paltz dance clubs. I went once, suffered a kiss from Gio, and realized that the biggest age difference in the world might be between twenty-three and thirty.

I kick him, and he hands over a ten. We both join Edi at the window.

This project was Gio's brainchild; it grew out of his senior thesis. He's got so many great ideas, but I can't help thinking that there's a reason most real-life projects aren't helmed by recent college grads. For instance, should we have installed all the doors upside down? Gio sees it as thwarting convention, but really, it's just wrong. We'll be able to wallpaper a room with all of our stop-work orders. "What do you think, man?" he asks Edi.

"I think you've got a lot to do," he says.

"We can always use help," Gio suggests.

Edi raises his eyebrows.

"He's got a job, Gio," I say.

"It's just the two of you in here?" Edi asks.

"Six," Gio says. "But the rest are grant-writing off-site."

Edi holds out a slip of paper with his name and number on it. "Call me next time you need a ride," he says to me, starting back for the stairs.

"You don't want to see the other floors?" I ask. "We already poured concrete down on the ground level."

"I should get going," he says. "I just didn't feel right about letting you come in here alone. Doesn't look very nice from the outside, you have to admit."

I smile. This is what my father would say, too. I take Edi's number.

I stay late, ripping out floorboards to make up for the time I lost in the morning, so it's been dark for hours by the time I leave. Hoist the chains and padlock up and around the factory's door handles, clicking them into place. Rotate my stiff shoulders, zip my jacket to my neck, and stare out onto the completely empty street. A train chugging up the Hudson, a fire truck blaring. I'm hungry, exhausted, and tempted to call Edi for a ride home, but of course, I can't afford to have him drive me every day. What would Patti Smith do?

I make plans to track down a bike soon. Daydream about banana seats and woven baskets as I power walk through the night. After a few minutes, I'm convinced someone's following me. I tell myself I'm being paranoid and press on. When I finally venture a look over my shoulder, though, there's a scrawny dude gaining on me by the second. Maybe he's just cold, but every self-defense class I've ever taken says to trust your instincts, no matter how judgmental those instincts might be. I duck into the Italian restaurant on the next block.

I know I should leave when I see that the guy's gone, but the place smells so good. Sorry paycheck and DWI be damned, I sit and order a plate of lasagna and a glass of red wine.

The place is charming—more bakery than restaurant, with white wrought-iron tables and a glass counter full of cold cuts and cannoli.

A couple of college kids on an ironic date in the corner and a few tables of older couples who've probably been coming here for ages. My lasagna is so hot I scald the top of my mouth on the first bite; it immediately begins to peel. I'm almost in tears when it cools down enough for me to appreciate the creamy ricotta and the stretchy mozzarella—Claire can never have this again? What kind of life is that? I order two cannoli and eat them both for dessert.

I throw a card down when I'm finished, but the waitress, an elderly woman with round gray hair like the cap of a microphone, tells me it's cash only. She gives me directions to the closest ATM, but I can't face going out there alone again. WWPSD? "I'll call a friend," I say.

When Edi pulls up, I lean in the front window and say, "Can I borrow twenty-five bucks?"

He lets me sit up front with him. "Is this allowed?" I ask.

"Who's going to tell?"

The first person we pick up is a young mother with hair down to her waist and a milk-stained shirt. She buckles her sleeping baby into his car seat and slides in next to him. She's already closing her eyes as she gives Edi directions in Spanish, and he takes off.

"How many languages do you speak?" I ask him.

"It depends how you count," he says.

We take the woman to a block that fills me with low-grade panic and watch as she enters a squat building. Someone who might be her mother kisses her on the top of the head. "What's the most frightening thing you've seen since you lived here?" I ask.

Edi presses his lips together, contemplating. "Well, I got stabbed in the arm," he says. "But my cousin did it. That could have happened anywhere."

I look at him sidelong, wondering if he stabbed back. "Could it?"

"You're scared here?" he asks. I notice he always uses his turn signal, pausing an appropriate amount of time at each stop sign.

"You were the one who walked me into my own workplace this morning," I say. "Shouldn't I be?"

We head over to the college next. Gio graduated from here last May and told me that if you follow the directions from the highway to campus on the college's website, you wind through the suburbs for forty minutes rather than take a ten-minute drive through the center of Poughkeepsie. Passing through the rest of Poughkeepsie before getting to the main gate does make the beauty of the campus almost perverse. It's an arboretum, for one; there are fairy-tale trees lining every path. Claire says she used to feel like a queen just showing up here for work.

"What do you think about this place?" I ask Edi. I don't know much about Albania, but I can imagine that if I feel a gnawing resentment here, he might have it worse.

"Nice," he says with a shrug. "I like driving around, looking at the architecture. The only thing is, you've got to be careful." He gestures at the kid who's just wandered in front of the cab, oblivious, with headphones on and a hood pulled over his eyes.

The main building that looms just beyond the gate is from the mid-nineteenth century, gabled, with wings stretching in either direction as if welcoming the students in for a hug. We pick up four girls, who wedge into the backseat, smelling of tequila and incense. Edi starts for the train station before they even ask him to, and we listen as they alternate between discussing a guy that two of them have been sleeping with and the contemporary relevance of Marxist feminism. They tip Edi twice what I would expect.

After dropping them off, we sit at the train station. Edi shows me the trick to reclining the seat. Then he rolls down his window and lights a cigarette. It's late enough that there's a lot of time between trains: an off-hour in an in-between place. Poughkeepsie's a city that grew up on whale rendering and then on IBM. There are still computer people here, but their numbers are dwindling. There's a revitalization effort down at the waterfront, but in the rest of town, every other house seems to have a weather-battered "For Sale" sign in the yard. And the college kids? Except for a few like Gio and the rest of my coworkers, trying on blue collars and taking a little too much pride in rolling up their sleeves, they never even know they're here. Edi's telling me about the restaurants in town he's grown to like—a Jamaican place that makes coconut bread, a Chinese takeout where you can order off-menu—when I notice that a police officer is making his rounds, on foot, nearer and nearer to the cab on every pass through the parking lot. He's portly, with a double chin, not the same officer from the other night but equally humorless, it seems. The third time I see him, I say to Edi, "What's up with him?"

"I think he thinks we're . . . you know," he says. "You know."

"No, I don't know," I say. "What? I can't take any more trouble with the law."

Edi doesn't want to say, but I figure it out when he blushes.

"Oh, great," I say. "He thinks I look like a prostitute?" I point to my work boots. "He obviously can't see my shoes."

"Maybe that's not what he thinks," he says. "I didn't mean to imply anything about you."

We sit, Edi smoking, me watching clouds pass across the moon, until even the police officer loses interest. Edi stubs out his cigarette on the side of the cab and says, "You know André Kertész? The photographer from Hungary?"

"Vaguely," I lie.

"There's a famous photograph he took of this train station. You moved here for a pop star, and all I knew was that picture. My cousin sent it to me as a postcard. I thought, at least if there's a train station there, I can go anywhere."

Edi and I pick up Claire from the hospital the next morning. The doctors didn't quite want to let her go yet, it seems, but her crappy insurance said four nights in the hospital was plenty. I'd been sleeping for only a few hours when she called to say they were discharging her. I'd brought the steak knife to bed with me but was so tired I slept straight through all the scary night sounds. I can't imagine that Edi slept at all, but when he shows up at my curb, his hair is freshly combed and he's wearing a different shirt. I worry that I'm costing him money when he comes in with me rather than find another fare, but he says he doesn't mind. Claire is a picture of diminished capacities even in her fixed-up, dischargeable state, but he doesn't flinch. He takes hold of her flimsy arm, helping her down the hall.

"Is this the hospital you came to when you got stabbed?" I ask him. Claire's eyes flit between us; she has no idea, yet, who he is.

"Same cousin who stabbed me sewed me up," he says.

We settle into the backseat of the cab. Claire says, "The one good thing is that I'm not cleared to fly. My parents couldn't get me back to Colorado if they tried. Stuck in Po-Town."

As he drives us to our place, Claire rests her head on my shoulder. Edi rounds the civic center, makes that left turn on red, and continues up the road.

CHEM HASKANAM

When he was a boy in Iran, my father avenged the death of a flock of pigeons by dashing out the brains of a cat. He'd made pets of the birds, fed them stale lavash. Their throaty coos were a comfort. Seeing them afterward—wings separated from bodies, bits of beak and talon in the yard—was not the worst example of sense-less death he'd live to see, but it was the first.

Even to a child, it was clear that the cat, self-satisfied and cleans-ing itself of feather fuzz with its small tongue, was the perpetrator of the crime. It wasn't easy to catch, but my father was determined. He used milk and a stone, each cupped in a palm.

When I see the parakeet on the sidewalk, my father's old story flashes through my head. That depth of feeling for birds never made sense to me. Not until I see this one. It's the same color—spring green—as the inside of a just-snapped pea. It drops down in front of me as if falling from the sky. If not for its constant jittery movement, I might have dismissed it as a leaf.

I throw my arm in front of Vartig so he doesn't take another step. "Look down," I cry.

"Look up," he responds, nodding at a nearby tree. Among the dark leaves, brighter specks shimmer: parakeet friends. He carries on down the street.

I tell him to wait. I have the perverse desire to catch one, to possess it.

"They live here," he says. "I see them all the time."

I stretch my hand toward his elbow but can't get a grip. He reaches into his pocket for his keys.

This is my first time at Vartig's, even though we've been together three months. After earning his doctorate from Brooklyn College, he kept stubborn residence in an apartment near campus. He teaches robotics now, but what started as mere convenience persists as a badge of honor. Manhattan isn't even a glimmer on the horizon; his neighborhood might as well be a foreign country. He thought I was being xenophobic the first time I said that. For two children of immigrants, we spend a lot of time nitpicking each other's prejudices.

"I'm talking in terms of hours," I explained. "In the time it takes me to get out to your place, I could fly to Paris."

"I'll take you to Paris," he said.

And I believed him, although our careers—professor and librarian—don't suggest that jet-setting is in our future. We did meet out of town, though, at a bizarre little bakery upstate, near Poughkeepsie. He was there to give a talk at the local university, and I was visiting a friend for her birthday. I'd called in my order, and when I gave my name at the register, he looked up from his coffee to ask if I was Armenian. We discovered we both lived in Brooklyn, and the coincidences, at least to me, seemed divine. I might not have thought so if he'd revealed exactly where in Brooklyn he lived, but we didn't get much further than wonder-struck stares and the exchange of phone numbers. I returned to my friend's place with two surprises: the birthday cake and the announcement that I was in love. Of course I believed we'd go to France. How like me: I even bought a dress I thought would look romantic against the backdrop of the Tuileries.

So I complain about his neighborhood, but it's not that I've refused to come; he's never pressed me. Or, if I'm being totally truthful, he's never even asked.

I've been to Paris before, though. When I was twenty, I spent a semester studying there. I learned next to no French and socialized exclusively with other Americans. Studying abroad is wasted on college students. I could have been anywhere but for the extra ten pounds of croissant weight and the fact that my aunt Dina, my father's sister, and her husband, Yves, lived across town in one of the fancier arrondissements. After the family left Iran, she landed in France while my father wound up in the States; growing up, I saw her so rarely that it was a luxury to be only a Métro ride away.

Twice during my six months in Paris, Dina and Yves conned me into going to church with them. The first time, they left me a message with only an intersection, a place to rendezvous on a Sunday morning. I assumed I'd find a café there and they'd buy me a tartine. When I arrived to see their stout figures waiting for me on the ornate steps of an Armenian church, there was nothing I could do but kiss-kiss their cheeks and squeeze between them in a pew. French? Armenian? Latin? I spent the next hour or six without a clue what I was listening to.

In the courtyard after services, the motivation for their invitation became clear, as Dina introduced me to all the single male parishioners as "Anahit, *la petite américaine.*" The men were all too young or too old, too square or too French—all, that is, until she brought me around to the priest. I'd been zoned-out during the service, but up close, he was magnetic. Handsome and broad-shouldered, he stared straight into my eyes. Even in his religious getup, this guy was *chaud.* When he took my hand and said, *"Enchanté,"* I swore I'd learn French.

Despite my crush, I didn't go back to church until a few days before I left Paris. My sublet had ended, and I was staying with my aunt and uncle. There was no graceful way to avoid attending services with them. I knew, at least, that they couldn't try to fix me up with anyone, not with my flight booked two days later. Dina did lecture me on the way over—"It's like you speak *fewer* languages than when you arrived!" I tried to say that they, too, were insular when they lived in Iran with only other Armenians, but the parallel was weak. "You have so many options, Anahit," she said.

So I sat there, breathing in the smoky incense, watching the theater of church unfold around me through layers of homesickness. I couldn't wait to get back to the States, but I also missed Paris in anticipation of leaving. I missed my aunt, too—even though she was there next to me, even though I didn't know that I'd never see her again. In my head, I chanted the only Armenian words I knew, a phrase my father taught me when I was small: *Chem haskanam.* It means "I don't understand."

Years later, after I told my parents about Vartig, my father asked, "Did you let Dina know you're finally dating an Armenian?" It took us all a moment to remember why I hadn't.

Vartig and I sit cross-legged on the floor of his monastic apartment. When it's clear that I won't let the parakeet issue go, he tells me that, first of all, they're really dwarf parrots and they're descended from an Argentinian shipping crate that overturned at JFK back in the 1960s.

"Or that's what everyone says," he continues. "To me, it doesn't make sense. What about the climate change, diet, the stressors of urban life?"

At this, he rubs his eyes, which are long-lashed and wary. They are the eyes of my cousins, of the boys on the Armenian General Benevolent Union's mailers—folded brochures I find in my mailbox no matter where I move.

"I don't know what I'm talking about," he says. "Never mind."

I'm ready to head back outside, now that we've dropped off my overnight bag, stuffed with a variety of impractical items I'd gathered from my dresser in a rush after Vartig discovered he'd forgotten the pills he takes for his irregular heart and we'd have to go to his place to get them. "I've got to take some pictures."

He leans over and presses his forehead against mine. "Anahit," he says, "every eighteen-year-old art major at Brooklyn College has done a photo essay on those birds."

I sleep in stops and starts on Vartig's punishingly hard mattress. That Parisian priest makes an appearance in my dreams. One day maybe I'll be visited by a vision of Dina and we'll get to talk, but for now, it's only ever the priest. And we're never in church.

In the morning, Vartig's standing at the window, backlit by the sun, a white towel around his waist. "Did your family ever talk about eating caviar for breakfast in Iran?" he asks.

I pat my hair down from the unruly heights it achieved overnight. "Yours too?"

"Can you imagine?" he asks.

"I've never had it," I say.

"I haven't since I was little," he says. He sits down beside me on the bed. "I took a bite, and it popped between my teeth in this way I didn't expect. The taste was so fishy. I spit it out." He reaches his hand into the thicket of my hair, mussing it skyward again. "My father hit me across the mouth."

"Oh no," I say.

"It was the only time he ever did something like that. We'd just moved to LA. He must have been looking forward to sharing a spoonful of caviar with his son," he says. "And I ruined the moment."

"You were just a kid."

"I bet as an adult I'd like the stuff. But I haven't tried it again."

"Brighton Beach!" I cry. "We're not too far, right? Let's go. I bet we could find some in those Russian grocery stores."

"I just said it was a bad memory, Anahit," he says. "Why would I want to do that?"

He takes his small round pill from the orange bottle beside the bed and places it on his tongue. He swallows without water. One day, he may need surgery. Maybe he'll get a robot heart.

I push the covers off my legs, pull the towel off of him, and head with it into the bathroom. I let the shower run hot and step in. I replay our conversation in my head. He lets me think we're speaking the same language, then makes sure that I know we are not. He wants only as much connection as he wants.

I lean forward, searching for my reflection in the steamy mirror. It is impossible to define: a photograph taken too close.

I can't decide if my parents would like Vartig. My mother would certainly find him handsome, although his arrogance wouldn't escape her. And my father, while he doesn't trust robots for a second, does like to see a successful Armenian. He had these riffs he'd go on when I was small and even more gullible. According to him, Armenians were first on the moon. Confused, I'd ask why the flag up there wasn't red, orange, and blue.

"We're a modest people," he'd say.

My mother, shaking her head, would stifle laughter.

"Think about Mount Ararat," he'd continue. "Noah's ark landed smack in the middle of Armenia, but you don't hear us saying we're responsible for all of humanity. It's not like we spend our time going on about it, even though it's spelled out in the Bible." He'd open up the Old Testament and show me, right there, the proof. "We're God's people."

While I was in the shower, Vartig pulled on black pants, folded into cuffs, with a navy T-shirt, rolled at the sleeves. He sits on the love seat with his boots on the coffee table, his arms behind his head. His hair is close-cropped on the sides, longer and brushed back on top.

He looks like he's relaxing after a day doing something insidious—patrolling a fence, barking orders. He is cold and beautiful. If I told him he looked like a fascist, I could ruin his day.

But sometimes it's as if I worship him. Like I'm guilty of idolatry.

"Did you go to church when you were little?" I ask, tucking yesterday's shirt into my bag before sitting beside him, balancing on the arm of the couch.

"Of course," he says. "Isn't that the first question other Armenians ask you when they see your last name: 'Where'd you go to church?'"

"My father went to the potlucks sometimes, but we never did. My mother's influence—she's this total Upper West Side atheist."

"I forget you're only half," he says. "Because your hair is so dark. Take it down from that ponytail."

I tug out the rubber band. The smell of his shampoo fills the room. He grabs me and pulls me onto his lap, holding my head back to kiss my neck. His lips brush my throat as he asks, "So do you believe in God?"

"What a question," I say. Beyond him, the window frames the day—sunshine and endless sky. No tall buildings block the view. I feel the flutter of wings in my stomach.

"Are you looking for the parakeets?" he asks.

"See," I say. "Sometimes you do know what I'm thinking."

"Oh, go find them if you want." He says something more, something in Armenian, his face softening, as if he's invoking a secret we share.

I cup his face in my palms and reply, "*Chem haskanam.*"

The neighborhood is quiet on Sunday morning, just distant church bells and the sighs of a kneeling bus. The birds, too, must still be asleep. I wander onto the college campus, sit on a bench, and call my father. "I've been thinking of your story about the birds."

He's quiet for a moment. "I don't know what you're talking about," he says.

"The pigeons," I say. "In your garden?"

"Oh, you mean the ones I stoned," he says. "They were always bothering my cat. Have I ever told you? She used to drink milk right from my hand."

I start to laugh. How like me, to get the story all wrong.

CASSIOPEIA

Joe snaps a long branch where it forks. Evelyn watches him break the wood but still startles at the crack. Already on their morning hike, she's issued two false mountain lion sightings. He hands her half the stick to help navigate the steep path. It's time to head back down.

Surrounded by a fragrant thatch of low-hanging pine branches, Evelyn can hear the boys before she sees them. "That howling is your friends, right?" she asks Joe. "Not coyotes? Not wolves?"

Despite her fear of the wild, the members of Joe's playgroup, all Colorado-born, have let her know that nature does not truly exist here on the East Coast—that these trees, these hills, these mists and winds are not God's best work. A passable draft at best. They look at her, a native New Yorker, as if she's responsible for all of this, or at least as if she would defend it. The night before, she told them that growing up, nature was Central Park. "Real wilderness? That was Brooklyn."

Now she and Joe emerge from the woods. As Evelyn wipes a viscous patch of sap from her palm onto the tail of her shirt—this is her first time in flannel and hiking boots—Carl, Luis, and Ravi come into view. From this distance, frolicking with a Frisbee, they move like a unit, all wiry muscles and exuberant shouts. Men without women. They look fully themselves. Evelyn's mere presence precludes Joe from taking part. As they get closer, he reaches up to catch the disc, but it zips by him again and again.

The playgroup—she should probably stop calling them that—grew up together; this camping trip is a tradition. Carl's girlfriend, a sporty college senior named Allie, demanded to come this year, hence Evelyn's invitation to join. When Allie bailed last minute, Evelyn tried to bow out, too, but Joe convinced her she wouldn't be intruding. "My friends will love you," he insisted. But they probably feel like they have their mother along, and they're taking it out on Joe. She retreats to their tent.

When Evelyn was these boys' age, ten years ago, she was nothing like them. She didn't even know anyone like them. At twenty-four, twenty-five, her boyfriends were vampires, subsisting on buybacks and cocaine. They were more anarchists than altruists. Joe, on the other hand, started his tech nonprofit, Switchboards, before finishing college. Carl's an EMT, and Luis served as a medic in Afghanistan. Even Ravi, with his penchant for indie rock and his sleeve of tattoos, interns for a public defender.

She digs out a bag of smoked almonds, eating them by the handful. They make a paste in her dry mouth, so she has to take a begrudging drink. Everyone's purifying their own water with tablets and something that looks like an IV bag. She doesn't trust the system at all, but once she starts drinking, she can't stop, emptying the bottle. She tries to sit still after but has visions of tiny tadpole parasites wiggling through her veins.

Yesterday evening, while Joe stoked their campfire to life, the boys laughed at her when, marveling at the white density of the stars, she kept trying and failing to pick out the W of Cassiopeia or Leo's curved tail. They laughed even harder when she produced the pricey stash of frozen shrimp she'd brought for dinner. "If you're going to eat seafood out here," Luis said, "it should be fresh-caught."

"But we haven't had time to go fishing," she said.

"If we eat those, we'll be puking all night." Carl seemed to think his EMT training gave him a measure of authority.

"They were frozen, and now they're perfectly defrosted," she argued. "It's the same as taking them out of the freezer and leaving them on the counter until dinner—they've just been in the cooler instead."

They didn't buy it, so she took the soggy bag in her hands and sulked away, deflecting Joe when he came after her. Sitting on a log under all those stars, she'd pitched the shrimp into the lake. It had been petulant and immature, but she couldn't help it. Now, as she stares at the olive surface of the water, a small fish drifts into her field of vision: silvery, floating on its side, cloudy-eyed, a shrimp tail emerging from its mouth.

"You're kidding," she says aloud.

She crouches to get a closer look, praying that this shrimp is a different shrimp, perhaps one that exists here naturally. Up close, though, it is clearly peeled. She scuttles to retrieve her walking stick and reaches for the fish, first trying to sink it, then, unable to gain enough purchase to push it down, to nudge it back from the shore, out of sight. It stays put at first, hovering within view, but finally floats to the middle distance, visible only as a glint on the water.

She hears a commotion behind her. The boys have all stripped down to their boxers and are charging into the lake. Joe heads straight for her. They're screaming and cheering and kicking up fountains of water, and she knows she's about to be tackled. She half wants to let it happen, to laugh and let go, but she can't stand the idea of soaking these clothes; Joe bought them for her—the "hers" versions of "his," which nearly killed the playgroup when they first saw them—and they're the only woodsy things she owns. She dodges Joe, and then

Ravi, who tries to grab her as he leaps by. She sprints until she's out of reach.

"She's a fast one," Ravi says. He's talking to Joe, but he's looking at her.

"I had no idea. That's the most athletic I've ever seen you, Leela," he calls.

Evelyn flinches when he calls her Leela; she imagines him projecting a different, more confident woman onto her outline. She pretends to flex her muscles.

There's something sweet about the way the boys are in the lake, their hair sticking up, bellies bare. She loves the freckles on Joe's neck, the taut muscles of his lower back. Carl and Luis jump like fish, throwing themselves out of the water and going nearly horizontal before flopping back in. She's mesmerized for a moment, watching them. Luis has a network of scars running down the side of his chest that twist and shine as he moves.

"Come in," Joe begs. "It feels good, I promise."

She shakes her head, not wanting to ruin their moment in the water. But Joe keeps at her. Despite the autumnal chill of the morning, she's sweating under her layers. They're in a strange dog-day extension; Joe promised orange leaves—full fall splendor—but the trees are still holding fast to their green. "In my underwear?" she asks. She never would have thought to bring a bathing suit in October.

"We're in ours," Joe says. "No one cares. We'll close our eyes."

"I won't," Ravi teases. Luis and Carl exchange a look.

"Don't be gross," Evelyn says. "I'll come in, but seriously, do something else for a minute."

She wonders, again, what Joe knows about her fling with Ravi. It was fleeting and before she met him, but she can't figure out if Joe's never mentioned it because it's inconsequential or because he doesn't know there's anything to mention.

"Okay, okay." Joe puts his hand on Ravi's shoulder. "Let's give the lady her privacy." He rears up with a whoop and knocks down his friend, holding him under. They wrestle and thrash around for a moment before paddling off to join Carl and Luis, who are tossing a football a few yards away.

Evelyn digs loose the double knots of her boots and struggles to pull her jeans over her damp feet. Standing pantsless, her plaid shirt hanging down to the top of her thighs, she reaches for her top button and pauses. These twentysomethings have never seen dappled skin, blue veins, thighs like hers. She's done nothing to earn her marred body, not like Luis. She's a musician, a quiet part-time indie rocker, at that—she hasn't lived hard. She wakes up at seven every morning to go to an office job. For all the gigs she's played over the last fifteen years, she doesn't have much to show for it. No scars but also no fame, no acclaim, no swagger, no strut. With her clothes on, she may not look so very different than the girls these boys sleep with, the ones they slept with before her, but this is another story. At least she's wearing plain black underwear and a cotton bra, nothing sheer or lacy. She finishes unbuttoning the shirt, places it on top of her jeans, pulls her undershirt off in one swoop, and turns back toward the water.

Of course, everyone is watching. "What the hell," she cries. Her instinct is to laugh, even though she doesn't find the situation funny. She wants to take off in the other direction or at least straight into the water, but no way is she going to run, bouncing and jiggling—no way. She can't help sucking in her stomach. "Joe," she says. He holds his arms out, grinning.

The water swallows her. She skims under the surface, shaking off the shock of the cold on her chest, and swims for him. She keeps her arms outstretched, blows bubbles from her nose, hopes her breath will hold until she reaches him. Her lungs burning, she feels her fingertips strike skin, the solidness of a stomach, and she surfaces, face-to-face with Ravi. She's gone off course.

"Well, hello," Ravi says, trying to hold her above water, his hands under her arms. She feels the pressure of his palms as she pulls in air and the heat of the sun reflecting off of his face.

"My hero," she says, twisting away.

Last spring, Ravi brought Joe to one of her shows—a true disaster in which she wound up on a bill with a punk band called the Sacraments or something, and most of the people there to see her were too scared to stay for her set. The boys didn't bail, though, and Ravi sought her out after she played. She was happy to see him again, but when he introduced her to Joe then slipped away to talk to someone else, Evelyn understood she was being handed off. She was furious only until Joe said, "I held my breath while you were singing." They'd exchanged numbers by the time Ravi returned.

Ravi's still holding her, her back against his bare chest. She lets him do the work to keep her afloat while her heartbeat slows. As she treads, she can feel him pressing against her just a little harder. His breath tickles her neck.

Then Joe grabs her by her upper arms and dunks her. Cold water forces its way up her nose and into her mouth; it tastes like mud. Coming up sputtering, she knees him in the stomach, then flails her legs, kicking Ravi. "Get out of my face," she hiccups. "Seriously."

Joe yelps in pain, and the shine of glee in his eyes dulls. "We're just playing," he says.

"Because you're children," she says. In the stare-down that follows, Evelyn wonders if she's done it. Was that finally mean enough? He folds in on himself. She'd gone into this trip with the expectation—not the hope but definitely the expectation—that he'd break up with her afterward. Every moment she's had with him up until this point has been tinged with that fear. Will this be the day he realizes he could meet someone more like him? How could he not recognize, at some point, that they're stamped for expiration? It was almost a relief when he invited her camping, something she knew she'd be a terrible sport about. She thought, *How could we possibly survive that?* Now that they're in the midst of the weekend, though, she can't follow her own logic. He won't discover anything about her out here that he didn't already know.

Or will he? She eyes him and Ravi. She should have said something right away—months ago—but she didn't want to seem like she'd sleep with any and every twenty-four-year-old who stumbled into her audience. Especially if Joe was only going to be around for a week or two. But by four months, five months, six months later—too much time had passed. Of course, there's the distinct possibility he's always known. Lost in circular thoughts, Evelyn bicycles her legs to stay above water. A floating shrimp tail bobs by. She plucks it out of the water and tucks it under the elastic of her underwear so it can't resurface.

Evelyn is floating on her back, humming the beginning of a new song and planning an apology for her outburst, when she feels a disturbance in the water beside her. She jerks upright—her first thought is that it's a snake. But it's just Luis, sly and serpentine. "Why does Joe call you Leela?" he asks.

"He thought that was my name," she says. "I always rush through introducing myself. Now he jokes that it's my alter ego, the person I am onstage. I think he likes her better."

"Like you have multiple personalities or something," Luis says. He gestures from Joe to Ravi, from Ravi to Joe.

Evelyn feels a seasick flip in her stomach.

"What?" Luis asks. As he swims away, he calls, "I didn't say anything."

One by one, they leave as the lake starts to chill. Evelyn is the last one out. Joe meets her at the shore with a towel extended by way of apology. She rests her head against his sharp collarbone as he rubs warmth back to her arms. They're barely dry before Luis suggests another hike up a steeper trail than the morning's. He asks her if she brought a book.

"I did," she starts to say before interrupting herself. "Wait, why?"

"It just might be a little rough for you," he says.

"Hey," Joe says. "She'll be fine, man."

Luis gets a wry look on his face, his mouth twisting to the side. He says, "What about you? It's a tough trail."

"Don't worry about it," Joe says, his feet planted apart and a falsely bemused expression on his face. "Let's get going before it's too late."

"I'll stay behind," Evelyn says. She is surprised by how vocal Luis is about not wanting her around. For all her fears about not being good enough, she's rarely had them so clearly confirmed. "I'll be okay."

Ravi comes up next to her. "Don't worry about it," he says into her ear, lips skimming her skin.

"There's obviously some issue," she whispers back.

"Not with you," he says. "Swear."

Luis snorts and reaches out to nick Joe in the arm. "You going to do something about the two of them?" he says, lifting his chin toward her and Ravi.

In vain, Evelyn wills her cheeks not to color. Ravi steps back, his jaw slack. Joe grabs Luis's shoulder, hissing something into his ear. She says, "I'll fuck all of you, if you're worried about missing out."

Joe laughs hard enough that she can tell he doesn't find it funny. If she weren't nervous about staying out here alone—people do get mauled by mountain lions; she's read articles to prove it—she would crawl into their tent, pull the sleeping bag over her head, and stay there until they were ready to go back to civilization.

Instead, they set out—Luis and Carl up ahead, Ravi in the middle, Joe and Evelyn in back—marching in silence through the woods, which are probably beautiful, if anyone had been looking. It isn't long before Evelyn is having trouble keeping up. Her thighs get weak, and her breathing is shallow. She starts humming quietly to distract herself, to keep calm and propel herself forward.

"What is that?" Carl asks.

"Oh, I don't know," she says. She hadn't realized anyone could hear. "Just what came to mind."

"Sing it," he says. "These two are always talking about your killer voice."

"Any requests?" she asks. She sees Ravi start to turn, then pretend not to hear.

When no one answers, Joe says, "Luis, learn any marching songs in the army?"

Luis throws back a glance. "That's what we were doing over there," he says. "Singing."

The silence is brutal. At last she returns to the song she was humming, the one she's been piecing together ever since they arrived in the woods.

Pine needles to palms, sticky and sweet,
I lick the blood and brush back my hair.
If I fell from the hill, would you turn back for me
Or leave me in the mountain lion's care?

When she runs out of words, she starts over again, her voice expanding into the space of the woods. After a few minutes, they hit a patch of loose rocks she isn't sure she can manage. She reaches out to Joe for help, but he is already a few yards ahead, arm around Ravi's shoulder, deep in conversation. No one had been listening to her sing. She turns, carefully backtracks a few feet to a more level spot, and balances herself against a large cool stone.

Ravi is the one to realize she's no longer following. She sees him nudge Joe, who tries to slow everyone so he can come back for her. Luis and Carl keep their weight pitched forward, as if settling back onto their feet would be defeat.

"Wait up," Joe calls over his shoulder.

"Wait up, wait up," Luis chants, his voice high and mocking.

Joe turns slowly to face Luis, and the two of them step toward each other, stopping only once they're standing so close their chests nearly touch. The scene is absurd; they're like rams locking horns. Evelyn doesn't understand how it escalated so quickly, with so few words. Why are *they* the ones fighting? She catches Ravi's eye. "Break it up," she pleads.

"Don't talk to him," Joe barks. "I don't want you talking to him."

"Excuse me?" she says.

Then Luis punches Joe square on the jaw. Joe counters with a punch in the stomach, and Luis cracks him on the side of the head, his knuckles leaving four white marks. Joe skids down the rocky path, his body jolting as the stones catch him in his back, his neck, his head. He lands only a few feet from Evelyn, but Carl's already bounding down the trail to get there first. He crouches over Joe, whose body is bent at unnatural angles. Blood pours from his split lip all over his chin.

Carl holds his balled-up plaid shirt to Joe's lip with one hand and does a cursory examination with the other, poking extremities to see if anything is broken. Evelyn nudges her hand in place of Carl's, keeping pressure on Joe's mouth so that Carl can attend to the rest of him. "Can I put my vest under his head?" she asks.

"Don't move him," Carl snaps.

"My head's fine," Joe says, his voice garbled by blood and shirt. "I'm going to get up."

"Stay the fuck down," Carl says.

Ravi is standing over him now, too, reiterating what Carl says. "Don't move, dude."

"He didn't hurt me that bad," Joe says. Evelyn relaxes her pressure on his mouth so he can get his words out easier. "I was just surprised."

Luis's face is expressionless, taking in the scene. He stands with his arms clasped behind his back, a step behind Ravi, who makes himself wide—legs planted, shoulders squared—a wall between Luis and Joe. Joe's downplaying his injuries, Evelyn thinks, to make this all look less bad for Luis.

"How are we going to get him down?" she asks.

"Luis and I are going to get under each of his arms," Carl says.

Luis steps forward, nodding.

Ravi blocks his way. "No way, man," he says. "You're not touching him."

"It's okay," Joe says. "Ravi, it's okay."

"I got this," Luis says. "I got him."

Luis and Carl ready themselves, hands under Joe's back, his head, his arms. On the count of three, they lift him to his feet. He grimaces and sways. They hold him still for a moment, waiting for his dizziness to pass.

Even with Joe suspended between them, Carl and Luis are faster than Evelyn can manage. Ravi hangs back, keeping pace with her. "He'll be okay," he says.

The shadows falling across the path have begun to blend together with evening, growing indistinguishable from night. The boys up ahead disappear around a bend. Ravi switches on his flashlight.

"Was that because of me?" she asks, stepping even more gingerly now, in the near dark. She feels ridiculous asking.

"No," he says, without hesitating. "I'm pretty sure Luis has wanted to do that for a long time."

"But why?" Evelyn asks.

"You know Joe almost enlisted with him," Ravi says. "They used to talk about it all the time, the two of them. Luis followed through, but then, sort of out of nowhere, Joe started the computer-exchange thing. He arranged for *one* kid to get a used computer, and then, all of a sudden, it was Switchboards. He stayed to run it instead. He said he just needed a little more time, that he'd still sign up, but—"

"Are you saying that's why he started the company?"

"If you ask Luis," Ravi says, "Joe needed an excuse to stay behind."

Evelyn takes in a deep, piney breath, feeling a reordering taking place in her thoughts. Could he ever have been serious? She can't see him taking orders or falling in line, much less wanting to fight.

Ravi nudges her to speed their descent. Her eyes strain against the twilight. He takes her elbow so they can move faster down the incline.

"I have to ask," she starts. "When you and Joe came to my show—"

"He swears he forgot," Ravi says.

"He knew about you and me?" she asks.

"I asked him to come that night because I felt weird just showing up. You and I hadn't talked in a while. He told me afterward that it slipped his mind, the fact that we were there so I could see you. He wouldn't have asked for your number otherwise."

Evelyn should feel disappointed. She should think that Joe is dishonest and maybe even unkind to move in on his friend like that. But that's not what she's thinking. She's thinking that Joe knows what he wants. And what he wants is her.

Still, there is a moment between Ravi kissing her and Evelyn pushing him away. She remembers what it was like to be with him. "You were the one who didn't call me," she finally says.

He turns back to the path. There is a spark in the darkness, as if his flashlight is reflecting off a small glassy eye. "I think we should go back," he says. There is a tremor in his voice that escalates as he starts to move. "Hurry!"

He's faster than her, but Evelyn tails him as closely as she can, hoping to stay within sight. She's not sure if she is chasing or being chased. Her ankles threaten to turn on the rocky descent, but she plummets toward camp without slowing or stopping. Ahead of her, there is Joe in a folding chair, holding the shirt to his bleeding lip, the others hustling to pack up. When she reaches the clearing, she turns, squinting out into the pines. All she can see is the outline of trees and, above them, the radiant sky, full of stars.

META WALL

There's a girl in the after-school program Tess teaches who won't sit on a chair. She is not a small child but a teenager. As Tess sees it, there's no excuse. But in her experience, there usually is one, whether she sees it or not, so she lets Lolly pace while the rest of the class sits around the table.

They brainstorm ideas for the mural they've been tasked to paint on the outer wall of a little-seen corner of the school. The suggestions range from cryptic to bizarre. On the large piece of butcher paper between them, Thalia scrawls, in purple marker, "famous people." Fatimah writes "video shapes and colors." Rena taps her finger on Fatimah's thought and says, "Exactly." Lolly leans over Thalia's shoulder and adds, "Still looks like a wall."

"Four girls, three suggestions?" Tess asks. "That's all we got?"

They nod. It's amazing how sometimes they're in total agreement, without even glancing at each other, and other times the most mundane matters will leave them diametrically opposed. Trying to get them to agree on an arrangement for the tables in the room—pushed together in a square, a line, or a *U*—once drove Tess into the hall to compose herself.

"Okay, then," she says. "Lolly, will you take a seat with us so we can talk about these thoughts?"

"Nah, I'm good, miss," she says. She pushes a flyaway back into the high bun she wears most days and pulls her sweatshirt sleeves down over her hands. Fatimah and Rena roll their eyes. Rena mouths the word "crazy." They think no one can see them if they hold their scarves in front of their faces. Tess ignores the attitude and asks them each to explain what they wrote.

"The people who've graduated and gotten famous," Thalia says. She has a lisp and deep dimples that appear every time she speaks. "You know."

"No," Lolly says. "We *don't* know. No one ever got famous from here."

Tess would like to say that that's not true, but Lolly's got a point. The school has only been around four years, only graduated its first kids the year before. "Thalia," she says, "that will be a great suggestion for the students five years from now. When you all have had time to become stars."

Thalia snorts; she knows when she's being placated. Fatimah pulls some sort of electronic gadget out of her bag. Tess bites her lip—so hard it hurts—to keep from reminding Fatimah that those things aren't supposed to cross the school threshold. Fatimah hits a few buttons and shows the group a wild sequence of music video clips—the aesthetic of which is a cross between a screen saver, Op Art, and the tribal-print leggings the girls all started wearing this year. Neon factors big.

"Hot," they all say. "Hot."

"Lolly?" Tess asks, turning from the screen. "Can you explain what you wrote?"

"It would be cool to paint the wall to look exactly like it does now," she says, circling the table. "All the little stains and tags and chips of paint? I think it would seem sort of eerie to people, like something was different about it but they'd never know what."

"A meta wall. What a neat thought, Lolly," Tess says amidst the groans of the other girls. "Yoko Ono did a piece just like that at my college. Have you heard of Yoko Ono?"

The girls fidget, having hit their group discussion limit. Tess wants to ask them if they even know who the Beatles are. But she can't bore them too much—the administration won't let her continue this class if enrollment drops below four. The voting block of Fatimah and Rena guarantees an easy win for "video shapes and colors." Tess lets the girls watch the clips a few more times, zoning out herself, hypnotized by the chevrons and swirling outer space scenes. She passes out oil pastels and paper so the girls can start their own mock-ups. Lolly takes her materials over to the windowsill, standing to sketch. Tess watches her work for a moment, but there isn't much to see. Her drawing looks like everyone else's.

"I know exactly what's going on," Betsy tells Tess, swiveling on her barstool. "I think. What does she look like?"

"Normal girl," Tess says. "Long hair in a bun, big eyes. Okay skin. Sweatshirts, jeans, those ridiculous wedge sneakers."

"She's thin, though?" Betsy asks.

"Very," Tess says, finishing her drink—a variation on a piña colada that tastes delicious but so weak she glares at the bartender to see if he's trying to put one over on her.

"She's anorexic," Betsy says. "It hurts her butt to sit—no padding."

Tess abandons her evil-eyeing of the bartender, giving her full attention to her friend. "I should have thought of that," she says.

"I used to bring an extra sweater to sit on," Betsy says. "Although that was me in college. In high school, I was a total chunk."

"I knew there was a simple explanation for her bullshit," Tess says. "People act like teenagers are these mysterious creatures, but they couldn't be less enigmatic."

"I'm sure that doesn't make them any easier to teach, right?" Betsy is a lawyer, kind to give so much credit to Tess's work. Tess doesn't even have to do what real teachers do, prepping these girls for all those endless tests.

"It does, actually," she says.

"Men, on the other hand," Betsy says, pulling a folded-up sheet of paper from her purse. She smooths it flat and passes it to Tess. A simple question is written at the top left, in blue pen: *Are you wearing stockings?*

"What the hell is this?" Tess asks.

"From this prosecutor," she says. "Ross Grant? I've mentioned him before because—God help me—I thought he was cute. He passed it to me on the way into court."

"Did you report him?" Tess holds up a finger and steps up to the bar. She gestures at the new frozen-drink machine that appeared this week. The bar is too nice for something like that—it is tongue-in-cheek for them. The piña colada isn't really a piña colada but a drink that involves coconut *cream* and some sort of house-made ginger syrup.

"Do you know how to use that?" she asks the bartender. "I don't think you put any alcohol in." Even as she says it, though, Tess realizes she's leaning against the bar for support. She's a little drunk. "Never mind," she says. "Two more. We have a tab." Betsy is one of those successful friends who pays for drinks without comment—she'd handed her card to the bartender when they arrived.

"It's worse," Betsy says when Tess returns with the frosty glasses. "I wrote back."

"Jesus," Tess says.

"I wrote," she hiccups with laughter, "'Who am I, your grandmother?'"

Tess nearly falls off her stool.

"I thought it would put him in his place," Betsy continues, "but he started laughing. We almost got caught. And then"—she pauses and takes a thoughtful pull on her straw, her cheeks hollowing as she tries to get at the too-frozen drink—"and then, suddenly, it was kind of hot."

"Hot?" Tess asks. "I think he could have done a lot better. Sounds like he's totally out of touch with twenty-first-century fashion, for one thing." Of course, Tess wouldn't mind being passed a dirty note. Good luck in her line of work—the nonprofit arts-education world is hardly teeming with straight men. In her twenties, Tess lived with a self-styled "postmodern" graffiti artist, but that didn't end well. He became a lawyer after she moved out; Betsy runs into him sometimes. In a few years, Tess figures, she'll meet a nice divorcé.

"I don't know," Betsy says. "My therapist obviously would tell me to run."

"And that's why you're not telling her, right?" Tess asks.

Betsy tilts her head up, looking at the ceiling. Tess follows suit. There are molded Spanish-style details over the arched doorways and spare black iron accents around the walls, blue-and-white tiled floors, a few perfectly placed plants. She says, "I wish we could live in here."

Tess heads to school early, hoping to catch the guidance counselor. She avoided going through the normal channels—talking to her boss about Lolly wouldn't do any good. The organization she works for operates on this alternate idealistic plane; her boss would either contact Child and Family Services within moments or she would shut down the program—in any case, she wouldn't be helpful.

Even though she spends her afternoons teaching art in various schools and community centers, Tess hasn't gotten used to walking the halls of a high school as an adult. The first thing she notices is the smell. It's both antiseptic and too human, stuffy and salty with a chemical edge. Tumbleweeds of discarded homework drift across the floors, and the lights buzz in the drop ceilings. Despite it being last period when kids should be in class, there are quite a few of them roaming around, greeting each other with shoulder bumps and clasped hands. In Tess's day, there would have been an administrator on their asses, but the only adult she sees is the security guard by the front entrance. She shows ID, signs in, and asks for directions to the guidance office.

She sits on a bench, waiting for the counselor to finish up with whomever he or she is speaking to in there. After fifteen minutes, a kid slouches out, earbuds already inserted, and the counselor invites Tess in. She's small and round, about fifty, with close-cropped dark-red hair and glossy purple lipstick. Her miniscule office is piled floor to ceiling with books and paperwork. Her desk, though, is impeccable and spare.

"How can I help you?" she asks, in a faint Caribbean accent.

"I wanted to mention something I've noticed about one of my after-school students, Lolly Diaz," Tess starts.

Ms. Winsome sits up straight in her chair. "You've seen her?" she asks.

"Well, of course," Tess says. "In class, last week."

"But this week?" she asks. "You've spoken with her?"

Tess shakes her head. "I don't see them outside of the mural project."

"We haven't seen her since last Thursday," Ms. Winsome says. "Called home—nothing. No one's heard from her."

Tess's mouth goes dry. It's typical: she thinks she's identified a problem, only to realize she's ten steps behind. "What do her parents say?"

"Nothing," she says. "Well, I shouldn't say that. She doesn't live with either of them. I can't give you too much more. But let us know if you hear from her?"

"Of course," Tess says, and proceeds to think the worst.

The drinks are cherry-flavored this week—a Slurpee, if Slurpees featured locally sourced fruit and small-batch bitters. If Tess pouts, she can see her own pinked lips.

"Why would it be *your* fault?" Betsy asks.

Tess sighs. She means so little to these students that obviously it isn't her fault that Lolly is missing. Which makes it, she thinks, her fault.

"It's been two weeks now. I thought for a while that the other girls knew something I didn't, but I think they actually don't give a shit. They're so cold."

Fatimah and Rena, deploying their hijabs like clubhouse walls, froze out Tess and Thalia in equal measure. Tess spent class working with Thalia on her painting skills, showing her how to "dance her brush" so that she wouldn't leave streaks and could create the solid fields of color she was looking for. Sometimes she thinks Thalia's having a nice time, but she always wants to clean up five minutes early.

"My boss keeps trying to cancel the course," Tess says to Betsy. "I tell her that it would be horrible for Lolly to return from wherever she is to find out that the class was canceled because of her—that it might even be detrimental to the *case*, but I don't actually know if there is a case. No one will tell me. The guidance counselor says she can't relay any more information than she already has, which on a scale of one to ten is zero point zero."

"You're getting very worked up," Betsy says. "Please have another drink."

"Gladly." Tess asks for a plain old gimlet this time around, licking lime from the rim. "The whole reason I got this stupid job was to have time to paint, yet when I'm alone, I sit at the computer and Google 'Lolly Diaz' and try to figure out what happens to missing high schoolers. Do you realize what an issue prostitution still is in this city?" The gin burns her stomach. She hasn't gone grocery shopping in ages, eating only what she can grab at the bodega or the corner pizzeria. At thirty-three, she finally grasps that it makes a difference what she eats.

"Do I realize?" Betsy parrots. "You remember what I do, right?"

"You're probably defending the pimps," Tess says. She believes in the justice system and everything, but sometimes the people that Betsy defends—it can seem a bit deranged.

"No comment."

"Can you do some research?" she asks. Her stomach kills. It's not just the eating poorly; she is sick with worry over this girl. She can't shake the feeling that no one is looking for her. "Can you see if she's been arrested or something?"

Betsy nods. "No," she says, still nodding. "Can't use my resources that way."

"Thank you," Tess says. "I'm so grateful."

"While you're feeling so warmly toward me," Betsy says, "I should mention I'm seeing Ross again tonight."

Tess reaches across the table and slides Betsy's drink away from her. "Are you wearing stockings?"

Fall grows chillier, and Tess realizes she shouldn't have been puttering around with all the preparatory sketches; not only are the girls complaining about the cold but the sun is threatening to make its exit before they're halfway done with class. They've collaged together their drawings, so something from each of their ideas will make it into the final mural, and spent the last two weeks gridding the mock-up for transfer to the wall. Now they stand facing it, their backs to the mostly empty parking lot, wind pummeling the sides of their faces.

"Miss, I'm supposed to get on a ladder?" Fatimah asks, jutting out her chin "Why don't you do it?"

Tess sighs before she can help it. She'd come in early to see Ms. Winsome, to find out if anyone had heard from Lolly, but the counselor wouldn't say. Who was watching over these kids? She was agitated even before she saw that the chill in the air had inspired Thalia to wear earmuffs indoors and Rena to blow her nose every ten seconds—usually in the direction of Thalia, who couldn't hear her, of course. She stares Fatimah down. "Whose mural is this, mine?"

"Yeah," she says. "You're the one making us do it."

Getting into this kind of back-and-forth with a student is never a good idea. Tess turns to Thalia. "You're up, then," she says, then repeats louder to be heard through the earmuffs.

Thalia tosses her hair and grips the ladder.

Fatimah, predictably, grows enraged. "But I designed the top part," she says. "She's going to mess it up. I want you to do it. *You,* miss."

It's clear now that Fatimah doesn't have a problem with the ladder—she thinks she'll mess up the painting. She's being so annoying because she actually cares too much, which makes her anything but annoying. Tess wants to hug her. She sends her up with a little extra encouragement, adding that they can always paint over anything they're not happy with, and busies the other two girls, on step stools, with laying in swaths of magenta, aqua, kiwi green. It's actually going to look really neat. For the first time, she has to stop the girls to clean up—no one has been watching the clock.

The next morning, her boss calls to tell her that the class is canceled. Enrollment has held steady at three kids for five weeks.

"Lolly is *missing,*" Tess says. "She didn't drop out of the class."

"I spoke with the school," her boss says. "She's not missing."

Tess braces herself against the kitchen wall, holding her hand to her chest. "They found her?"

"The grandmother requested her school records last week," she says. "She's fine. They moved back to the DR. It was apparently her caseworker's fault for not knowing who was and wasn't in the picture."

"Are they sure this is legit?" Tess knows in her heart that this isn't the end of the story. She can still sense the bad news coming. Someone's fooling them, and one day, maybe one day soon, she's going to see Lolly's face in some blurry yearbook photo flashing by on the news.

"You'll need to pick up the unused supplies from the school," her boss says, and then adds, like she's doing Tess a favor, "I'll put your check in the mail today."

Tess stares at her cuticles. She needs a manicure. Good luck on that without this job. Not that it was so lucrative, but the other residencies she has for the semester barely will cover rent. *Lolly's okay*, she says to herself, trying to believe it. She picks at a fleck of neon paint under her thumbnail. *That's all that matters.*

"I wouldn't mind being whisked off to the Dominican Republic," Betsy says.

"Do you think that's really where she is?" Tess asks. "You didn't turn anything up when you searched?"

Betsy shakes her head, stirring her drink with its straw. "I really did look. But hey. Here's my takeaway: I think you're too involved with these kids."

"I'm not involved at all," Tess says. "Class got canceled."

"That's sort of what I mean," Betsy says. "Like, either become a social worker or wait tables. Get in or get out."

"I was going to be an artist," Tess says. "I've been telling people that since I was six years old. I wish someone had let me know that what I really was going to be was a part-time after-school teacher or a barista. No one ever had the guts to say what you're saying." She leans back in her chair, watching the bartender muddle raspberries and mint sprigs.

"You can be so difficult. You know that's not what I said."

"That's what *I'm* saying, then. I give up."

Betsy waves at the bartender, ordering another round. "Starting over is a good thing," she says, raising her glass in a toast.

Tess is loading stacks of paper, oil pastels, and brushes into a granny cart when she hears footsteps behind her. Her first irrational thought is that it's Lolly. She turns to see Fatimah standing there, arms crossed.

"Rena said she saw you come in," Fatimah says. "And I said, 'Bullshit, because she quit.'"

"I didn't quit," Tess says. "Without Lolly, there are only three of you. My boss doesn't think it's worthwhile to pay for a class that small. I'd volunteer, at least until the mural's done, if she wasn't making me return the supplies. Honestly, you don't need me anyway."

Fatimah rolls her eyes. "That crazy bitch."

"When you run an organization," Tess says, "you really do have to think about money."

"I meant Lolly," Fatimah says, picking up some paintbrushes and zipping them into her backpack, a move that Tess watches with interest. "She stole this guy's bike, you know? And put it on the train tracks. When she was a freshman. Because he liked her too much, she said. Most girls get crazy when a guy *doesn't* like them."

Tess squints at Fatimah, looking for the lines between truth and fiction, if there are any with kids her age. Maybe it's *all* true. "I probably can't pack up the paint that's already open," she says. "My boss won't want it. I'm just going to leave it on the shelf."

Fatimah winks. "I feel you, miss," she says. "You think you're slick."

Tess winks back, then maneuvers the cart out of the closet, down the hall, and onto the cold autumn street. As she struggles to the subway, she detours to look at the half-finished mural. The colors stop at eye level, since they'd started painting from the top, except for a small portion to the left that Thalia, gone rogue, designed herself. It says, in thick purple brushstrokes, *We was here.*

SPEED DREAMING

When I hear the local newscast, I'm just finishing Buster's cake. He is turning three and finally understands what a birthday is, and that this time it's happening to him. There will be a kids' party this year, because he has friends now, friends whose parents we've been forced to befriend, too.

But before the report is even through, I stop piping icing. I call Dax, who is picking up paper cups, pointy hats, kazoos.

"Jesus Christ," he says. "Our park?"

"It was spotted skulking by the fountain around sunrise," I say, "and yet is not there now. The park's already reopened."

"So it's fine," he says. "So the party's on."

I bonk my palm to my brow, theatrical for no one's benefit. "Not fine! Not on! The coyote's whereabouts are now unknown!"

"Don't take it so personally, Meg," Dax says.

I hang up on him. I've been trying to do that more. It's probably nicer than whatever I would say if I stayed on the line. Buster's cake is yellow, and I was going to draw a monkey on it with blue icing, but instead I make a sad face, with Xs for eyes. Then I scrape all that off and eat it with a spoon.

Dax calls back. "I'm sure it will be fine," he says. "A coyote in Queens? I bet it was some jerk's dog who got off-leash."

"You want to tell that to Jack and Song when the thing eats little Maddie?" I ask.

"Buster's really excited about this party," he says. I can picture Dax's face falling—a sight I know well—the way he must be blinking hard and slow. "We can't take it away."

At that moment the birthday boy himself shuffles out of his room. I am still surprised when he appears like this after a nap. These are his first few weeks in a big-boy bed, one he can enter and exit on his own terms without any need for me to liberate him. "Happy birthday, baby!" he screams, fists raised.

"Here's the thing, then," I tell Dax. "You're going to bring your gun."

Animal-control issues aside, it is exactly the kind of day we were hoping for—warm in the way those last few weeks of September can be, when every autumnal burst of sunlight is all the more precious because it might just be the last. The air is full of the toasted scent of leaves. Fifteen balloons dance on strings tied to the tables, soon to be smacked by an army of toddlers.

Dax is standing on the high ground of a tree stump, surveying the scene. We'd reserved a picnic area near the edge of what is, sadly, one of the few parks in our Queens neighborhood, where a paved lot with a swing set passes for play space. Slung over his shoulder, in his pristine gym bag, is the gun. As a butcher, Dax decided he'd feel more connected or authentic or something if he started hunting. He wanted to participate in the whole process, he said. He applied for the permit, underwent a background check, bought the gun, and donned the orange knit cap, but he has yet to shoot so much as a squirrel. I find the whole thing somewhere between shocking and appalling, but today I ask, "The bag's unzipped, right? Easy access?" He nods solemnly, a man on a mission.

Buster is patrolling the perimeter of the picnic area, raising his shoulders and asking, "Where's Maddie? Where's Colin? Where's Jackson? Where's Dora?" These are all his classmates—besides Dora, as in "the Explorer," who he thinks is real.

What somehow hadn't occurred to us is that the other parents, too, would have heard about the coyote. Texts start pinging as soon as we're set up, asking which it would be: Were we going to change the party's location or the date? I rub my temples. This has already been a miserable week. Thursday, I'd been over an hour late to pick up Buster from preschool, and when I got there—I was already so upset—he stared at me coldly for a moment before running into my arms. The idea of disappointing him again is unbearable. What three-year-old understands "postpone" or "just packing up for now"? *Well, I think, it's not like all the parents could have heard about the coyote.* If anyone asks later, I'll say I accidentally left my phone at home.

I gnaw on an apple slice and toss a ball back and forth with Buster, my eyes skirting the periphery. At every rustle of leaves, at the passing of every jogger, I lunge for him. He thinks it's a game and that it's hilarious. He asks for cake. I turn to Dax. "It's been half an hour," I say. "I think we should go."

He rolls his head around on his shoulders. "Yeah," he says. "I guess we should."

Buster, generally oblivious to adult conversation, picks up on this immediately. He throws himself on the wood chips, arms and legs flailing so fast he looks like a toppled windmill. "Happy birthday, Buster," he wails. "Happy birthday!"

"Don't take it personally, huh?" I call over to Dax. "That thing is ruining my child's party."

Dax covers his face with his palm. He's counting to ten before responding, just like the counselor we saw that one time suggested. My throat feels hot and tight. We actually had fun planning the party. We inflated the balloons and made maracas and bongo drums for a mini–jam session. We Googled the hell out of allergen-free snacks.

We hired a babysitter so we could go buy presents together, and then we sat side by side, rather than across from each other, at a restaurant so dark we could barely read the menu. We killed a bottle of wine.

I grab onto the back of Buster's shirt, trying to lift him from the dirt. He wiggles free and starts to run. I get out in front of him, fake the kid out, and catch him before he makes it too far. He's faster and heavier than he used to be, that's for sure. Holding him in my arms, I can't help but remember what he was like as a newborn, impossibly small, sweet-smelling, and fragile. I'm panting and trying to pacify the violent birthday bundle with a kazoo when, out from a clearing between the trees, I see it.

Another family.

Immediately, Buster is back in business. He points and waves. "It's Ileana," he says. I feel a twinge of pride in the way he says this little girl's name, a name even the girl herself mangles into "Ih-wee-ana."

Ileana's hair is a tangled nest about her small pointed face, and her mother, Sari, is apologetic. Her hair hasn't seen a comb today either. "One of those mornings," she says, gesturing at her child. "Could barely get her to put on pants. And this one." She eyes her older child, a six-year-old boy brandishing a long scavenged stick. "Don't get me started." The dad, Carlos, is already over talking to Dax.

Dax and I aren't close with Sari and Carlos. They own a design firm together, and although one or the other of them picks up Ileana from school every day, they rush right back to the office; they're usually gone by the time I arrive. I'm pleased they're the ones to show up here, though. The couple of times I've met her, Sari's seemed flustered in a semiglamorous fashion—as if she'd rather be sitting somewhere with a glass of wine than dealing with her children—and although Carlos is wearing a bowler hat I can't say I approve of, he's very handsome underneath it, with dark eyes and a thick, rakish mustache.

"At least you made it," I say. "Brave folks."

"I thought we'd be the last ones here," Sari says, pinching the bridge of her nose. "Nice to know sometimes that I'm not as big of a mess as I suspect."

I study her for a moment. She has no idea.

"Your timing is perfect," I tell her, handing Ileana and Buster each a balloon. They cradle them to their chests and beam.

When Carlos asks where everyone else is, I hear Dax tell him that we must have put the wrong date on the invitations. "Luckily, you caught our meaning, somehow," he says. I can't tell if he's winking at Carlos or me. He's more relaxed, having eased into a seated position on the tree stump, his hand resting on the duffel at his side.

The kids, for their part, don't seem to notice that they are a party of three. Alexander, the first grader, has the two little ones corralled under a picnic table. They giggle maniacally as he runs circles around them, hitting them with his stick if they try to escape.

"Were you okay the other day?" Sari asks me. We're seated on a bench across from the kids, watching their antics.

At first, I can't place her question, but then I realize she's talking about Thursday, the day I didn't show to fetch Buster from preschool.

I'm distracted for a moment as Dax places his hand over his bag. I follow his gaze across the park, preparing to run. But he's looking at some passing cops, that's all—a pair of zoned-out police officers biking by. Sari watches me, brows raised, waiting for the story.

I try to relax. Dax and I were going to bring a cooler of rum punch to the party before a firearm was in the mix. "I was on the subway on my way to pick up Buster," I start. "I went back to work mornings, now that he's in school. Anyway, there was this man holding on to a pole in the center of the car. Suddenly, between stops, something happened. He just collapsed. Dropped straight."

Sari gasps. While I can't picture the man's face, not anymore, I can see the shape of him as he fell—a blur of blue jacket, neat beard, and barrel chest, the flash of a silver watch.

"He hit his head on the way down, on the side of one of the seats. He landed right at my feet, and he was bleeding."

"What did you do?" Sari asks, waving her arms at her son to convey I don't know what. He's popping balloons now, the little ones going crazy as each one erupts with a snap.

"Some other guy, another passenger, handed me a gym shirt," I say. What I don't say is that I didn't take it at first. *Me?* I'd thought. *It comes down to me?* "It smelled like sweat. I knelt down and pressed it to the guy's head. I kept asking him if he was okay, but he didn't answer."

"And then what?" Sari asks.

My insides lurch with residual adrenaline. "Someone used the intercom and told the conductor there was a sick passenger. He held the train at the next stop until the EMTs arrived. It all worked pretty smoothly, I suppose."

"Good thing you were there," Sari says, glancing at the cake. I stand up to find the forks.

"I'm afraid I didn't help," I tell her, pausing with the stack of plates. "I was bending over him, holding the shirt to the wound, and I felt . . . this will sound, I don't know . . . but I felt his dying breath."

It was like the air going out of a cushion, faint and finite. A wisp against my cheek.

"And that was it?"

"I didn't feel anything after that," I say.

"From hitting his head?" she says. "No."

"It must have been a heart attack," I tell her. "Or an aneurysm. His skin was gray. It was whatever made him fall, not what happened on the way down."

I look at my feet, the same shoes I'd worn that day—comfort clogs I'd never have touched five years ago—the same shoes that I'd discovered a small drop of blood on later that night. I decided not to wash it off, but now, somehow, it's gone.

We sing to Buster, who stands up on the bench and conducts his adoring chorus. I cut fat slices of cake. Dax tries to join us at the picnic table, but I hand him his piece and send him right back to his post. Sari and Carlos give us the briefest quizzical look before letting it go. The cake is dense yet crumbly, my first foray into addressing all the nut-frees, dairy-frees, this-frees, that-frees in Buster's peer group. I am contemptuous of those absent hive-prone children as I chew, although no one else lodges any complaints. *I'm better than this,* I want to say. I kiss Buster on the top of his sweaty head.

"Three years ago today," I tell him, "I was screaming bloody murder trying to get you born."

"Bloody murder," he says approvingly. Ileana repeats it, chanting as she stabs her cake.

"That's not nice to say," says Alexander, his face smeared with blue icing.

Like his son, Carlos has a fleck of icing on his face. I can't stop looking at his mouth. Sari turns to him but doesn't wipe it off. Instead, she says, "Meg was telling me how she tried to save a man on the subway this week."

"That's why you were so late Thursday?" he asks. When it was apparent I was more than my usual few minutes late and I wasn't answering my phone and Dax wasn't answering his—he was back in some restaurant's walk-in freezer with no cell service—the teacher called all of Buster's classmates' parents, trying to find us. Or, more likely, just letting everyone know who'd won the bad-parenting award for the day.

"Did you all think I didn't have an excuse?" I ask. Buster's school is filled with kids like him and parents like us, yet I can't help but feel that everyone thinks we're the least equipped. Like they can all tell that Buster caught us by surprise.

Sari blushes. "We're awful," she says. "But what else are we all going to talk about, you know? We've all got our things. You're the late one. I mean, what am I?"

"I wouldn't know what your thing is," I say. "Since I'm always late, I miss the gossip."

Sari smiles, relieved. "Anyway," she says, "Meg pressed someone's gym clothes to his head as he lay there bleeding. But he died anyway."

"Bleeding murder," Buster says, his mouth full of cake.

"She doesn't know that," Dax interjects. He hates hearing about this again—I can see it on his face, the way his eyelids droop, shutting me out—and it only happened two days ago. Anything that happened to me bores him. "She doesn't know for sure that he died."

I glance at the kids. They're listening but not listening—the cake is their top priority. "I know it," I say. "I do know."

"She felt his dying breath," Sari says. I look sidelong at her and her husband. Do they get off on car crashes, like in that movie?

"Speaking of gym clothes," Carlos calls over to Dax, "you headed there after this, man?" He gestures at the bag. "What gym you go to?"

"Oh," Dax says. "We'll see if I actually make it. Don't know that I'll need to work this off." He motions to his untouched cake.

"Daddy's gun is in there," Buster says. He forms a pistol with his thumb and index finger, points the barrel right at Ileana, and shouts, "Boom!"

The little girl looks alarmed. We all looked alarmed. "Buster," I say. "What does Mommy say about guns?"

After cake, I hoist the pièce de résistance onto a low tree branch, a hugely expensive Dora the Explorer piñata. It's filled with Hershey's Kisses, the most wholesome candy option at Party Time. Before I can get it fully in place, Buster approaches and throws his dimpled arms around it. Dora is just shy of his size, and their stomachs stick out in the same way. I don't know what I'll do when Buster loses that round belly, that jelly-bean shape. "I love her, Mama," he says. "Happy birthday to me!"

This is not Alexander's first time at a party—he knows what to do with a piñata. He's already got his stick ready, and he's getting impatient. "Honey, go over by Alexander," I tell Buster as I pry him off Dora and finish tying the piñata to the tree. "He's going to show you what to do."

Dax steps back onto his stump and pulls out his camera to snap some pictures. Carlos follows suit. I join Sari by the kids and tie a bandanna over Alexander's eyes. He squeals as I spin him in three circles. Buster and Ileana are delighted by the sight of Alexander all tied up. I point him toward Dora, and he heads straight for her, swinging all the while. On his second try, he hits her square in the head with a loud thwack.

I see my mistake register on Dax's face the moment before I hear Buster's scream. "No!" he cries, rushing Alexander. "Dora!"

I'm already on the move, intercepting Buster just before he gets cracked in the face by Alexander's stick. I take the blow on my hip instead and bite my cheek, swallowing whatever expletives threaten to come out. Alexander removes his blindfold. "I did it," he says.

Poor Buster is writhing in my arms, deep into his second, ultimately warranted, tantrum of the day, red in the face and bawling as Dax uses his pocketknife to cut Dora down from the tree. Sari tries to calm down Ileana, who is hyperventilating, nearly as upset as Buster at the sight of her favorite cartoon character's head being brutally bashed in. Alexander is arguing with Carlos, saying, "But Daddy, I almost got the candy!" every time Carlos tries to coax away the stick.

"I'll tape her back up," I say. "Mommy will tape her back together." Buster stares at me with wide, wounded eyes.

Carlos interrupts, his iPhone in his hand. "I just got a text," he says. "Apparently, there's been a coyote sighting in the park?"

Do we feign ignorance? We do. We gather the necessities—the better toys, the injured Dora—as fast as we can. I hold Buster in one arm, Dora under the other as I kick supplies into a pile. Sari has Ileana on her back, and she's pulling together their various discarded sweaters and scarves. Carlos asks his son to "act like a big man" and help the grown-ups.

When Alexander picks up the gym bag and pulls out the gun, I want to leave my body. I can't get to him fast enough, not without dropping Buster, not without causing a scene.

Alexander's face is a pure expression of wonder—eyes shining, mouth hanging awed and open. Before I can reach him, Dax is there. He's between the boy and the barrel, he's knocking the kid backward, he's got the gun, and he's zipping it back into the bag.

Dax ruffles Alexander's hair, then rubs his hands together, and I see it all pass through him, the panic, the frantic calculations. His stout figure is spring-loaded, his arms tensed, his gaze bouncing back and forth between the side of Carlos's head and the back of Sari's—did they really miss it? Buster's breath on my face is hot and furious. I would do anything to go back to the beginning, to try this whole thing again, to do better. I search the distance for some sign of the coyote, some sign that the real monster here isn't me.

"Sorry about that, buddy," Dax says, forcing a smile. "Buster wasn't supposed to see that. We'll do presents later, back at home."

Back at home, of course, we don't do presents. Buster is too exhausted to notice. Because they helped us carry the party supplies, Sari and Carlos wind up at our apartment, although at this point they probably would have preferred to be on their way. We put the little ones down for a nap on Buster's bed, and Alexander swipes at our iPad for only a few minutes before he, too, is asleep.

In the kitchen Dax climbs onto a chair to find our nice wineglasses. Usually, we drink out of jam jars. I open two bottles. "We'll drink both, right?" I ask.

"Did they believe we didn't know about the coyote?" he whispers, stepping back down next to me, smelling the bottle of red. "We did some real dancing out there."

"I don't know why," I say, "but I think they did."

We settle, the four of us, onto the floor around our coffee table, and I pour us tall glasses of wine. The rug we're sitting on is dotted with ground-in rice cereal and tiny Lego bricks. I lay my head on Dax's shoulder, and he places his hand on my knee.

"Your story about the subway," Sari says. "It made me think of this game we used to play as girls, Speed Dreaming."

"I played that," I say. "At sleepovers. Of course." Sleepovers—that strange childhood ritual. I remember fitful nights spent too aware of all the other bodies in the room. Now there is nothing better than those early mornings in our crowded queen bed: the soft ebb and flow of Dax's sleep, the sprawling abandon of Buster's.

"What is Speed Dreaming?" Carlos asks.

"You bend at the waist," Sari says, "and breathe fast—in, out, in, out. And then—poof—you pass out."

"You used to do that?" Dax asks, squeezing my leg. "Why on earth?"

"You faint," I say, "and it's like hitting 'Reset.'" I remember how it felt—the dizzy, dissociative rush, the giddy revival. "When you wake up, suddenly it's a new start."

ACKNOWLEDGMENTS

Speediest, dreamiest thanks to my editor, Ed Park; my fellow writers and first readers, Sara Weiss Zimmerman, Ella Mei Yon Harris, Lauren Waterman, Nicole Miller, Dan Degnan, Shelly Oria, and Liam Baranauskas; my *Underwater New York* coeditors, Helen Georgas and Nicki Pombier Berger; my teachers Lauren Grodstein, Julia Fierro, Victoria Redel, and Melvin Bukiet; Vassar College and the Sarah Lawrence MFA program; Lindsay Sullivan, for the song lyrics in "Cassiopeia"; my agent, Julie Stevenson; my parents, Jill and Vahram Haroutunian; my brother, Greg Haroutunian; and my husband, my favorite, Dan Selzer.

About the Author

Originally from New Jersey, Nicole Haroutunian received her MFA from Sarah Lawrence College. Her short story "Youse" was the winner of the Center for Fiction's 2013 short story contest. She is coeditor of the digital arts journal *Underwater New York*, works as a museum educator, and lives with her husband in Woodside, Queens.